Atlas for
The American Civil War

Thomas E. Griess
Series Editor

AVERY PUBLISHING GROUP INC.
Wayne, New Jersey

ISBN 0-89529-302-1

Contents

Foreword

For over a century, cadets at the United States Military Academy have studied the campaigns of the American Civil War in varying degrees of detail. Not until 1938, however, was a specially devised atlas used to support that study; in that year, T. Dodson Stamps, Professor and Head of the Department of Military Art and Engineering, initiated a project to develop an atlas to support Matthew Forney Steele's *American Campaigns*. From that time, the concept of a closely integrated narrative and graphical portrayal has been a feature of the course, The History of the Military Art.

In 1959, the unique two-volume *West Point Atlas of American Wars* by Brigadier General Vincent J. Esposito was adopted as a text at West Point. It served its purpose well. But as the course was modified to include more than purely operational military history, the treatment of the subject demanded compression and accommodation to course-long themes. These changes dictated development of a new text.

This atlas, designed to support the new text, *The American Civil War*, provides less detailed graphical treatment than the Esposito text-atlas, but it emphasizes the totality of the war to a greater extent. Two of the four authors of the text, Lieutenant Colonel Gerald P. Stadler and Major Arthur V. Grant, Jr., designed the maps which comprise the atlas. The Department is indebted to them for their exercise of ingenuity and care in preserving historical accuracy. In accomplishing that task, they relied heavily but not solely upon the important Esposito work.

The Department is also indebted to Mr. Edward J. Krasnoborski and his assistant, Mr. George W. Giddings, who drafted the maps. Mr. Krasnoborski, whose superior skills are everywhere evident in the work, supervised the entire drafting effort, rendered invaluable advice, and performed most of the cartographic work.

Thomas E. Griess
Series Editor

TABLE OF SYMBOLS

BASIC SYMBOLS

Regiment III

Brigade x

Division .... x x

Corps .... x x x

Army .... x x x x

Infantry .... ⊠

Cavalry .... ◹

Cavalry Covering Force .... • • • • • • •

Artillery .... ⊡

Artillery In Position .... ⊞
(Does not indicate type or quantity)

Trains .... ⛟

EXAMPLES OF COMBINATIONS OF BASIC SYMBOLS

Barksdale's Infantry Brigade .... ⊠ Barksdale
of McLaws' Division   (McLaws)

Stuart's Cavalry Division .... ◹ Stuart (−)
Minus Detachments

First Corps .... x x x / I

Rosecrans' Army
of the Cumberland .... x x x x / CUMBERLAND ROSECRANS

OTHER SYMBOLS

	Actual location	Prior location
Troops on the march	➡	⇢
Troops in position	⌢	⌢
Troops in bivouac or reserve	◯	◯

Troops displacing and direction ...

Troops in position under attack ...

Route of march .... ⇢ ⇢ ⇢ ⇢

Strong prepared positions .... ⊔⊓⊔⊓

Battle Sites .... ⚔

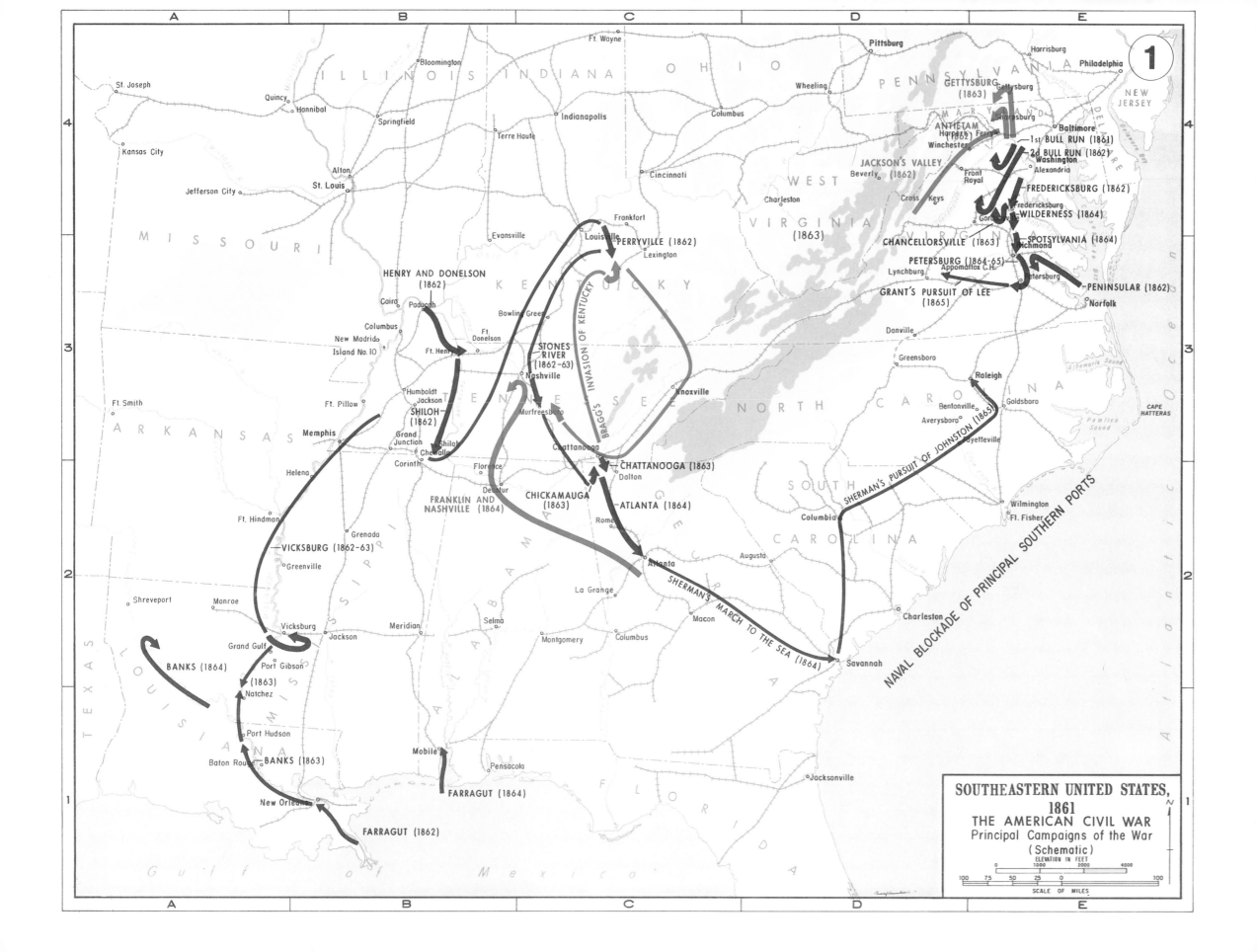

SOUTHEASTERN UNITED STATES, 1861
THE AMERICAN CIVIL WAR
Principal Campaigns of the War
(Schematic)

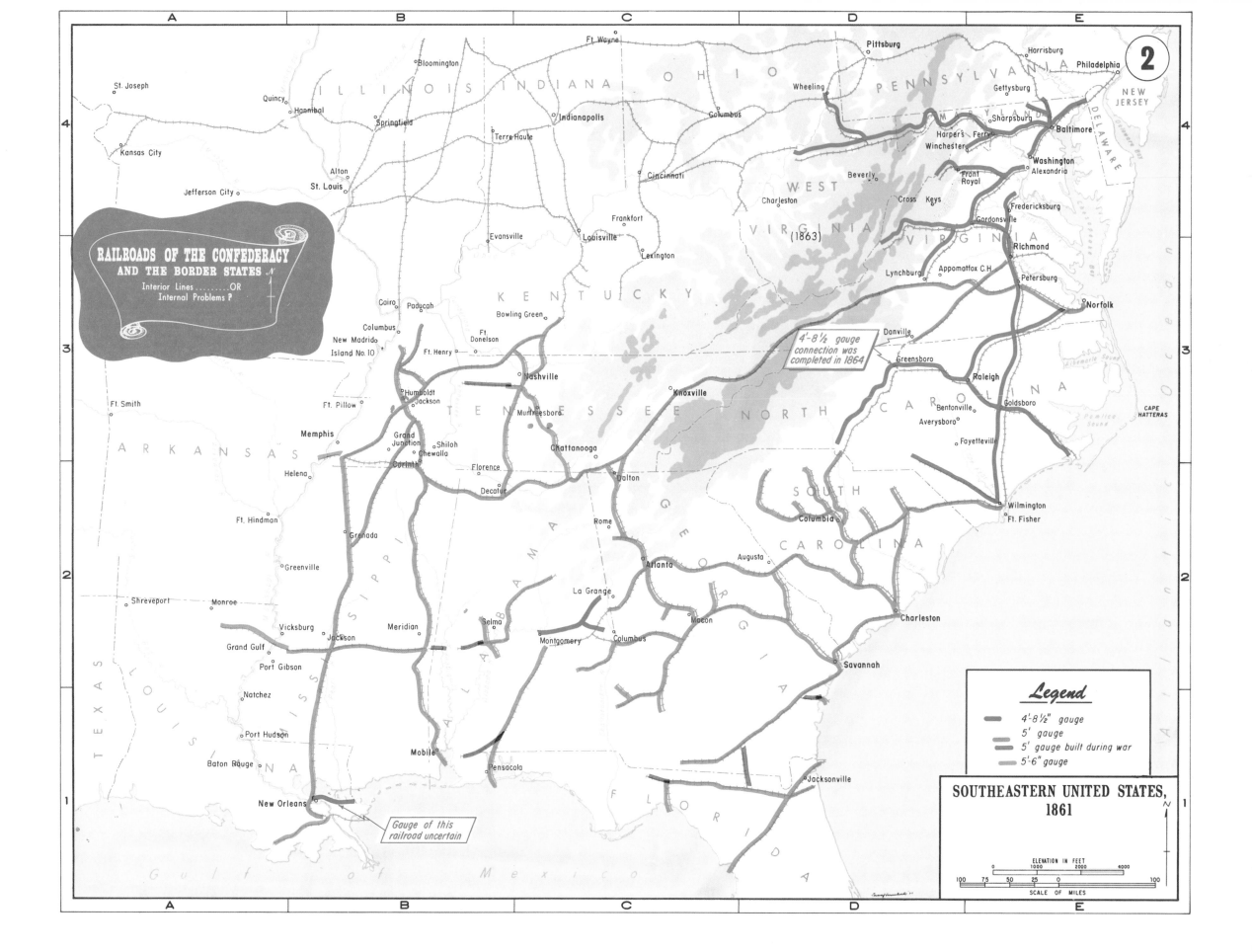

RAILROADS OF THE CONFEDERACY
AND THE BORDER STATES

Interior Lines..........OR
Internal Problems?

4'-8½ gauge
connection was
completed in 1864

Gauge of this
railroad uncertain

Legend

— 4'-8½" gauge
— 5' gauge
— 5' gauge built during war
— 5'-6" gauge

**SOUTHEASTERN UNITED STATES,
1861**

ELEVATION IN FEET

SCALE OF MILES

2

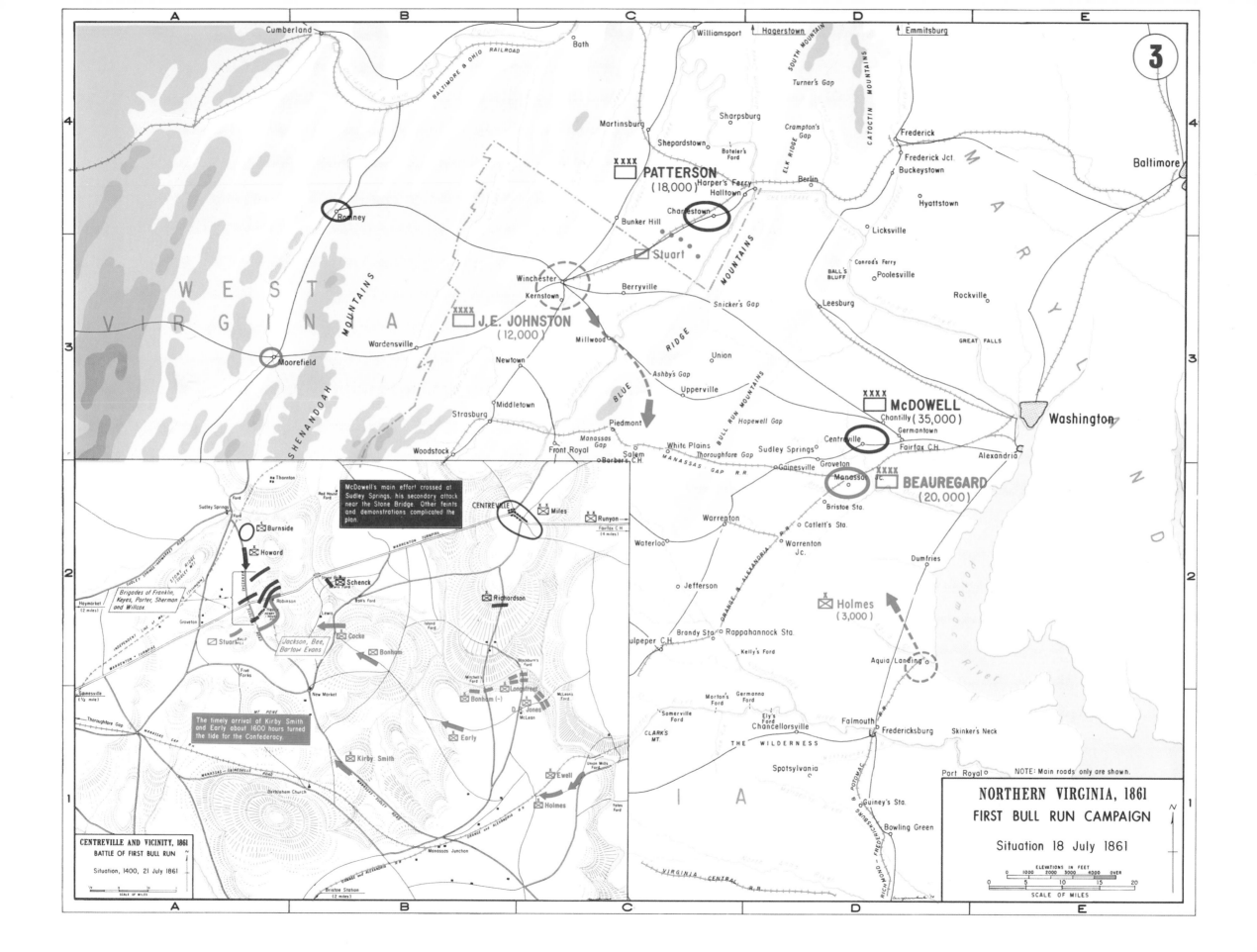

3

CUMBERLAND
Bath
Williamsport
→ Hagerstown
→ Emmitsburg
BALTIMORE & OHIO RAILROAD
SOUTH MOUNTAIN
CATOCTIN MOUNTAINS
Turner's Gap
Sharpsburg
Frederick
Martinsburg
Crampton's Gap
Frederick Jct.
Shepardstown
Boteler's Ford
Buckeystown
XXXX
PATTERSON
(18,000)
Harper's Ferry
Halltown
Berlin
Hyattstown
Romney
Charlestown
Bunker Hill
Licksville
Stuart
Conrad's Ferry
BALL'S BLUFF
Poolesville
WEST
Winchester
Berryville
Leesburg
Rockville
Kernstown
Snicker's Gap
VIRGINIA
MOUNTAINS
Moorefield
XXXX
J.E. JOHNSTON
(12,000)
Millwood
RIDGE
Union
GREAT FALLS
Wardensville
Newtown
Ashby's Gap
Upperville
Middletown
BLUE
Strasburg
Piedmont
Hopewell Gap
XXXX
McDOWELL
Chantilly (35,000)
Washington
Woodstock
Manassas Gap
White Plains
Thoroughfare Gap
Sudley Springs
Centreville
Germantown
Front Royal
Salem
Groveton
Fairfax C.H.
Barbers C.H.
MANASSAS GAP R.R.
Gainesville
Alexandria
Manassas
XXXX
BEAUREGARD
(20,000)
Bristoe Sta.
Warrenton
Catlett's Sta.
Waterloo
Warrenton Jc.
Dumfries
Jefferson
Holmes
(3,000)
Brandy Sta.
Rappahannock Sta.
Culpeper C.H.
Kelly's Ford
Aquia Landing
Morton's Ford
Germanna Ford
Somerville Ford
Ely's Ford
Chancellorsville
Falmouth
CLARK'S MT.
Fredericksburg
Skinker's Neck
THE WILDERNESS
Spotsylvania
Port Royal
NOTE: Main roads only are shown.

McDowell's main effort crossed at Sudley Springs, his secondary attack near the Stone Bridge. Other feints and demonstrations complicated the plan.

CENTREVILLE and VICINITY, 1861
BATTLE OF FIRST BULL RUN
Situation, 1400, 21 July 1861

Thornton
Red House Ford
CENTREVILLE
Miles
Sudley Springs
Ford
Runyon →
Fairfax C.H.
(4 miles)
Burnside
Howard
Brigades of Franklin, Keyes, Porter, Sherman and Willcox.
Schenck
Haymarket
(2 miles)
Richardson
Robinson
Gainesville
(1/2 mile)
Stuart
Jackson, Bee, Bartow Evans
Cocke
Bonham
Thoroughfare Gap
Longstreet
The timely arrival of Kirby Smith and Early about 1600 hours turned the tide for the Confederacy.
New Market
Bonham (-)
D.R. Jones
McLean
Early
Five Forks
Kirby Smith
Bethlehem Church
Ewell
Manassas Junction
Holmes
Bristoe Station
(2 miles)

NORTHERN VIRGINIA, 1861
FIRST BULL RUN CAMPAIGN

Situation 18 July 1861

ELEVATIONS IN FEET
1000 2000 3000 4000 OVER

SCALE OF MILES

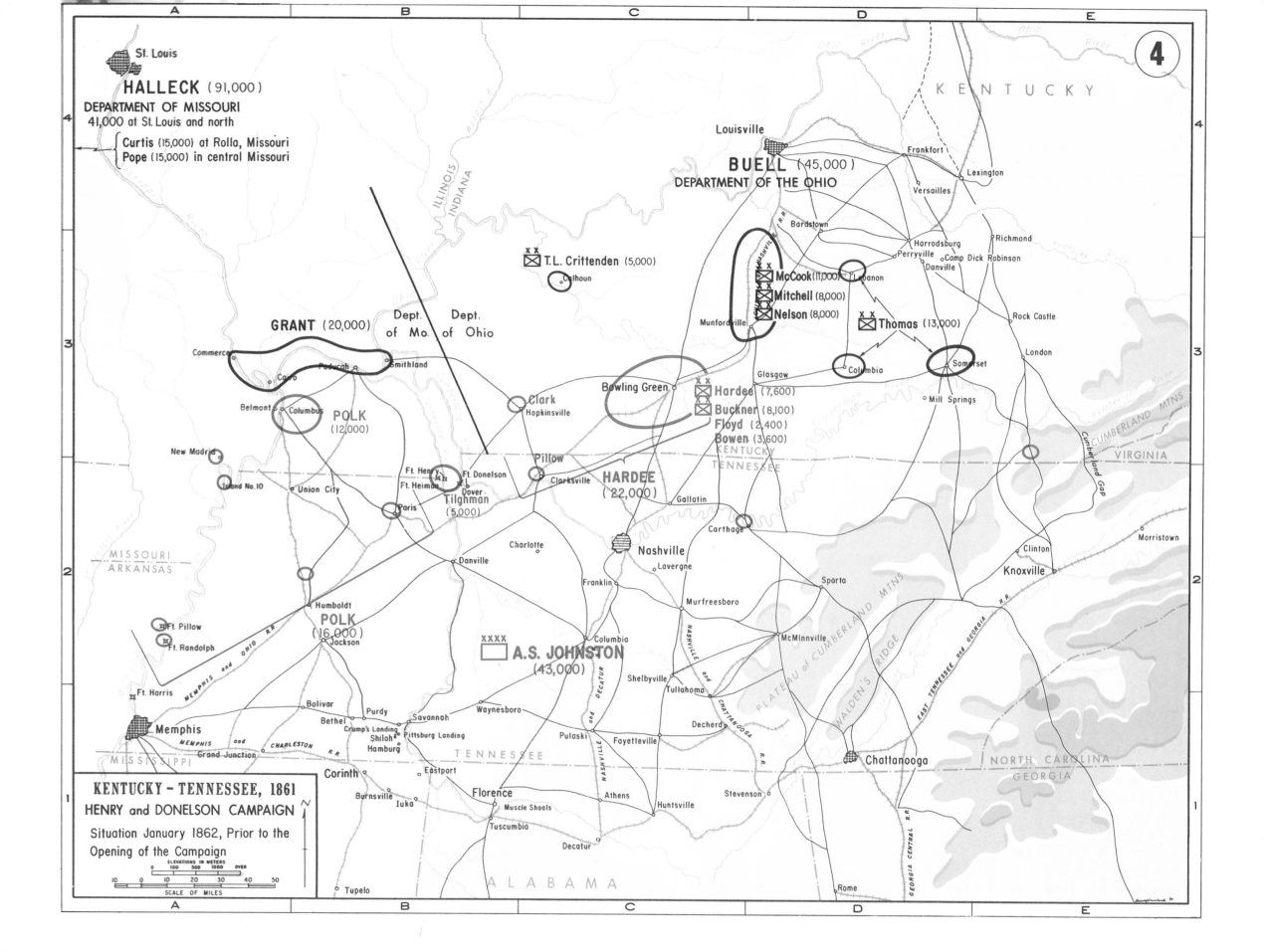

4

St. Louis

HALLECK (91,000)

DEPARTMENT OF MISSOURI
41,000 at St. Louis and north

Curtis (15,000) at Rolla, Missouri
Pope (15,000) in central Missouri

KENTUCKY

Louisville

BUELL (45,000)

DEPARTMENT OF THE OHIO

Frankfort
Versailles
Lexington

Bardstown
Harrodsburg
Perryville
Richmond
Danville
Camp Dick Robinson

T.L. Crittenden (5,000)
Calhoun

Munfordville
McCook (11,000)
Mitchell (8,000)
Nelson (8,000)
Lebanon
Thomas (13,000)
Rock Castle

GRANT (20,000)   Dept.   Dept.
of Mo   of Ohio

Commerce
Cairo
Paducah
Smithland

Bowling Green
Glasgow
Columbia
Somerset
London

Clark
Hopkinsville

Hardee (7,600)
Buckner (8,100)
Floyd (2,400)
Bowen (3,600)

Mill Springs

Belmont   Columbus
POLK
(12,000)

KENTUCKY
TENNESSEE

VIRGINIA

New Madrid

Pillow

Cumberland Gap

Island No.10   Union City

Ft. Henry   Ft. Donelson
Ft. Heiman
Dover
Tilghman
(5,000)

Clark
Clarksville

HARDEE
(22,000)

Gallatin

Carthage

Clinton

Morristown

Paris

Charlotte

Nashville

Lavergne

Sparta

Knoxville

MISSOURI
ARKANSAS

Danville

Franklin

Murfreesboro

McMinnville

Humboldt
POLK
(16,000)
Jackson

Columbia

A.S. JOHNSTON
(43,000)

Shelbyville
Tullahoma
Dechard

Chattanooga

Ft. Pillow
Ft. Randolph

Bolivar
Bethel
Purdy
Crump's Landing
Savannah
Shiloh
Pittsburg Landing
Hamburg
Waynesboro

Pulaski
Fayetteville

Stevenson

Chattanooga

NORTH CAROLINA
GEORGIA

Ft. Harris

Memphis

Grand Junction

Corinth

TENNESSEE

Eastport

Florence

Athens
Huntsville

MISSISSIPPI

Burnsville
Iuka

Muscle Shoals

Decatur

ALABAMA

Tuscumbia

Tupelo

Rome

KENTUCKY – TENNESSEE, 1861

HENRY and DONELSON CAMPAIGN

Situation January 1862, Prior to the
Opening of the Campaign

ELEVATIONS IN METERS
100 500 1000 OVER

SCALE OF MILES

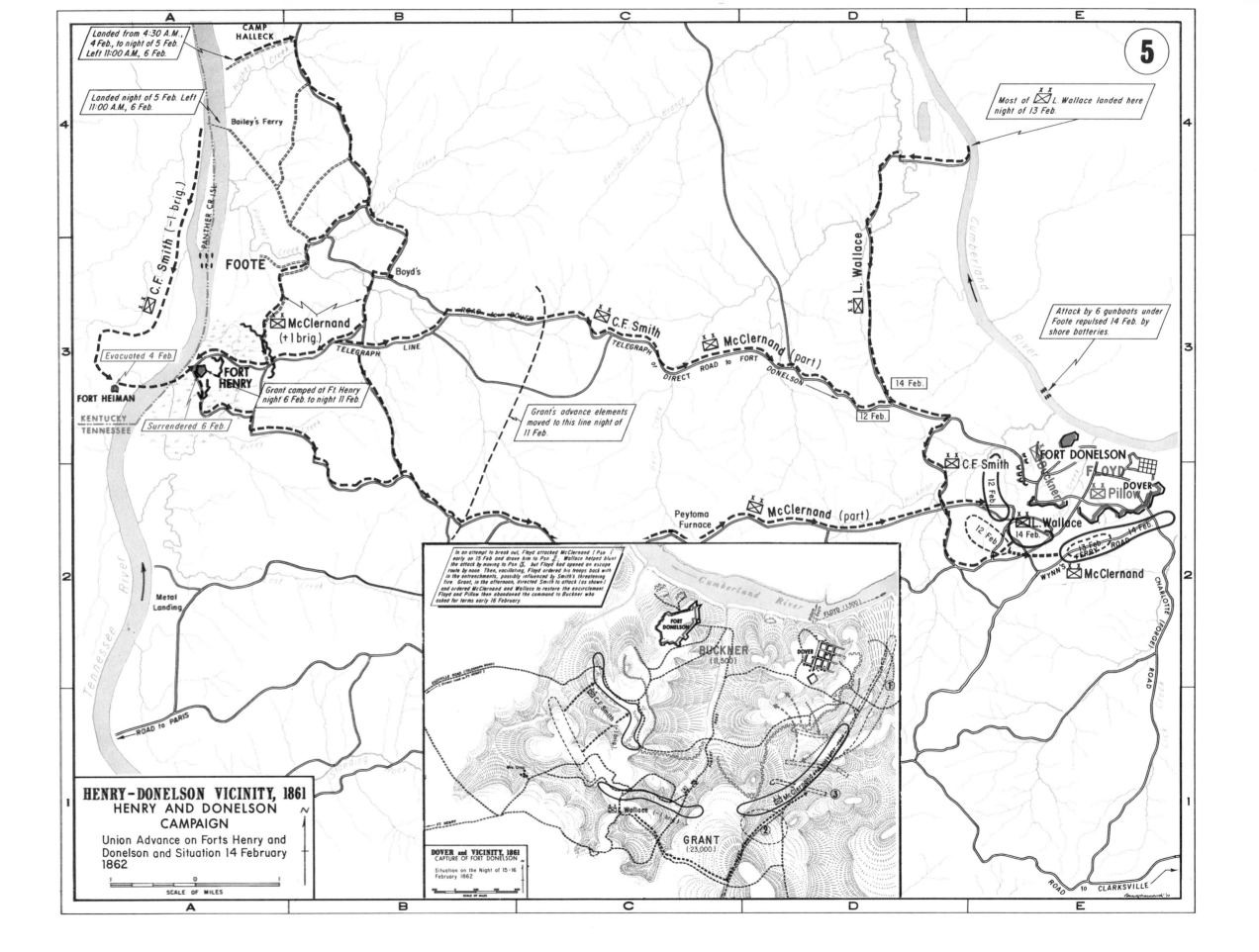

5

Landed from 4:30 A.M., 4 Feb., to night of 5 Feb. Left 11:00 A.M. 6 Feb.

Landed night of 5 Feb. Left 11:00 A.M, 6 Feb.

CAMP HALLECK

Bailey's Ferry

Most of ⊠⊠ L. Wallace landed here night of 13 Feb.

Boyd's

C.F. Smith (−1 brig.)

FOOTE

McClernand (+1 brig.)

ROAD now BOWER

⊠⊠ C.F. Smith

⊠⊠ McClernand (part)

TELEGRAPH LINE

L. Wallace

Attack by 6 gunboats under Foote repulsed 14 Feb. by shore batteries.

Evacuated 4 Feb.

FORT HENRY

TELEGRAPH

TELEGRAPH or DIRECT ROAD to FORT DONELSON

14 Feb.

FORT HEIMAN

Grant camped at Ft. Henry night 6 Feb. to night 11 Feb.

12 Feb.

KENTUCKY
TENNESSEE

Surrendered 6 Feb.

Grant's advance elements moved to this line night of 11 Feb.

FORT DONELSON

FLOYD

⊠⊠ C.F. Smith

DOVER
Pillow

12 Feb.

Peytona Furnace

⊠⊠ McClernand (part)

⊠⊠ L. Wallace

12 Feb.

14 Feb.

FERRY ROAD 14 Feb.

WYNN'S

⊠⊠ McClernand

Tennessee River

Metal Landing

Cumberland River

CHARLOTTE FORGE ROAD

In an attempt to break out, Floyd attacked McClernand (Psn I) early on 15 Feb and drove him to Psn 2. Wallace helped blunt the attack by moving to Psn (3), but Floyd had opened an escape route by noon. Then, vacillating, Floyd ordered his troops back within the entrenchments, possibly influenced by Smith's threatening fire. Grant, in the afternoon, directed Smith to attack (as shown) and ordered McClernand and Wallace to restore the encirclement. Floyd and Pillow then abandoned the command to Buckner who asked for terms early 16 February.

FORT DONELSON

BUCKNER (11,500)

DOVER

FLOYD (1,500)

Cumberland River

C.F. Smith (Teleg)

L. Wallace (−1 brig.)

FT. HENRY

GRANT (23,000)

ROAD to PARIS

HENRY–DONELSON VICINITY, 1861
HENRY AND DONELSON CAMPAIGN
Union Advance on Forts Henry and Donelson and Situation 14 February 1862

SCALE OF MILES

N

DOVER and VICINITY, 1861
CAPTURE OF FORT DONELSON
Situation on the Night of 15–16 February 1862

SCALE OF MILES

ROAD to CLARKSVILLE

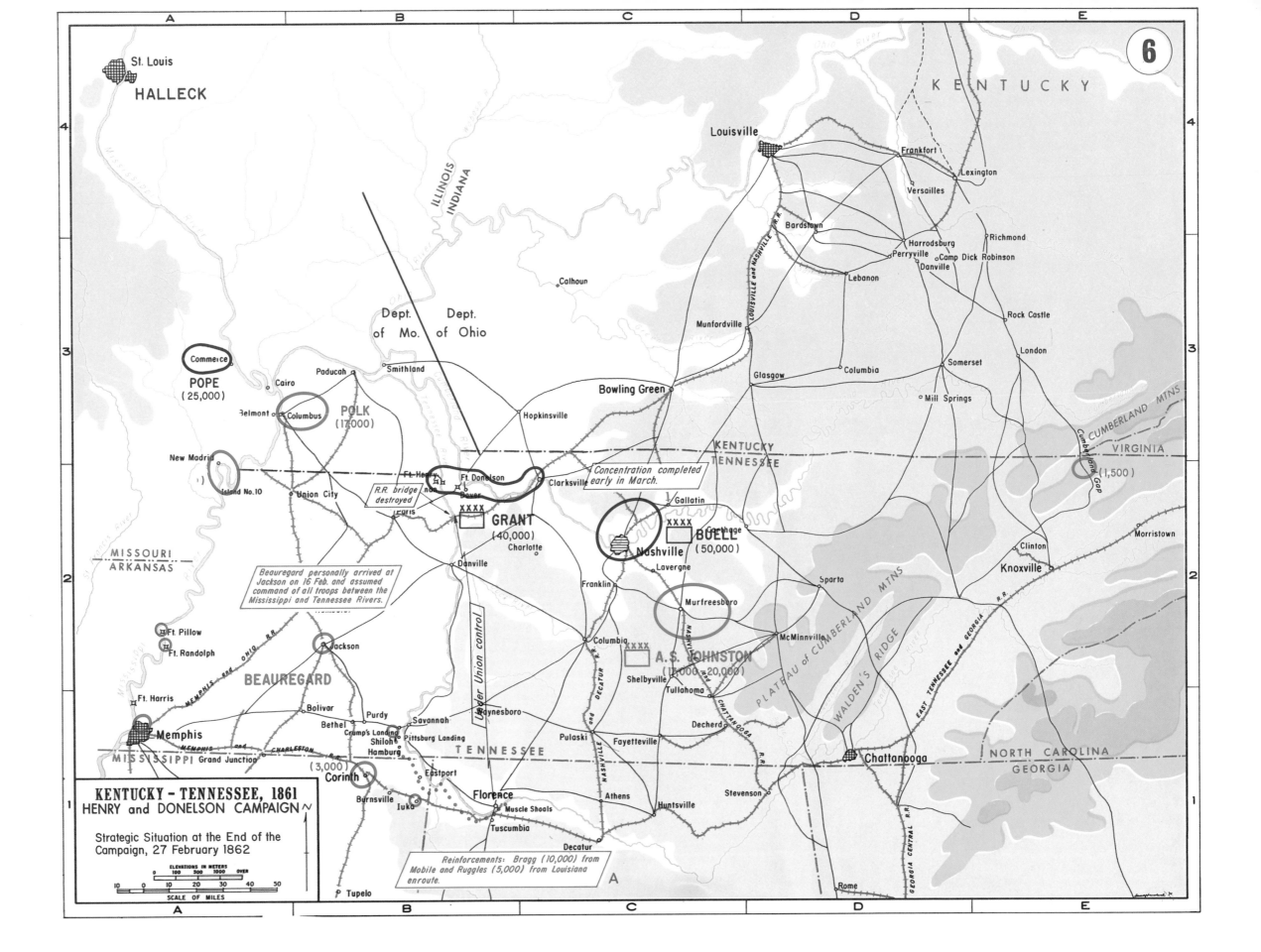

KENTUCKY - TENNESSEE, 1861
HENRY and DONELSON CAMPAIGN

Strategic Situation at the End of the
Campaign, 27 February 1862

ELEVATIONS IN METERS
100 500 1000 OVER
SCALE OF MILES

HALLECK

St. Louis

KENTUCKY

Louisville

Frankfort

Lexington

Versailles

Bardstown

Harrodsburg

Perryville   Richmond

Camp Dick Robinson

Danville

ILLINOIS
INDIANA

Calhoun

Dept.   Dept.
of Mo.   of Ohio

Munfordville

Rock Castle

Glasgow   Columbia   Somerset   London

Commerce

POPE
(25,000)

Cairo
Paducah   Smithland

Bowling Green   Mill Springs

Belmont   Columbus   POLK
(17,000)

Hopkinsville

KENTUCKY
TENNESSEE

CUMBERLAND MTNS

VIRGINIA

New Madrid

Ft. Henry   Ft. Donelson
Dover
Clarksville

Concentration completed
early in March.

Cumberland Gap   (1,500)

Island No.10   Union City

R.R. bridge
destroyed

Paris

XXXX
GRANT
(40,000)

Charlotte

Gallatin

XXXX
BUELL
(50,000)

Carthage

Nashville

Clinton   Morristown

Knoxville

MISSOURI
ARKANSAS

Danville

Lavergne

Beauregard personally arrived at
Jackson on 16 Feb. and assumed
command of all troops between the
Mississippi and Tennessee Rivers.

Franklin

Murfreesboro

Sparta

PLATEAU of CUMBERLAND MTNS

Ft. Pillow

Ft. Randolph

Jackson

McMinnville

WALDEN'S RIDGE

BEAUREGARD

Columbia

XXXX
A. S. JOHNSTON
(17,000 - 20,000)

Ft. Harris

Bolivar

Purdy

Savannah

Shelbyville

Tullahoma

Decherd

EAST TENNESSEE and GEORGIA R.R.

Memphis   Bethel
Crump's Landing
Grand Junction   Shiloh   Pittsburg Landing
Hamburg

MISSISSIPPI

TENNESSEE

Pulaski   Fayetteville

Chattanooga

NORTH CAROLINA

(3,000)   Eastport

Corinth

Burnsville   Iuka

Florence

Muscle Shoals

Athens

Huntsville

Stevenson

GEORGIA

Tuscumbia

Decatur

Rome

Tupelo

Reinforcements: Bragg (10,000) from
Mobile and Ruggles (5,000) from Louisiana
enroute.

6

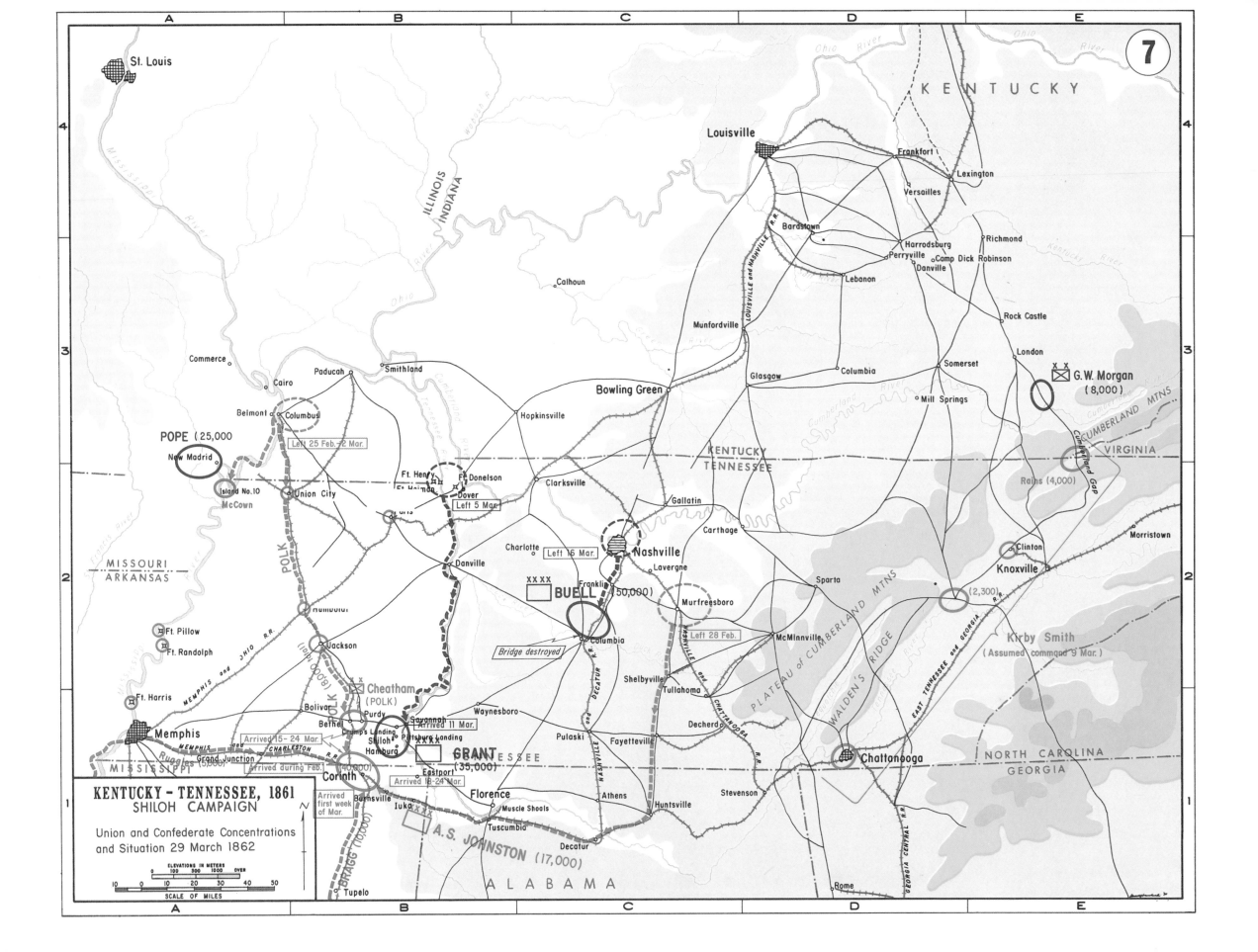

KENTUCKY – TENNESSEE, 1861
SHILOH CAMPAIGN

Union and Confederate Concentrations
and Situation 29 March 1862

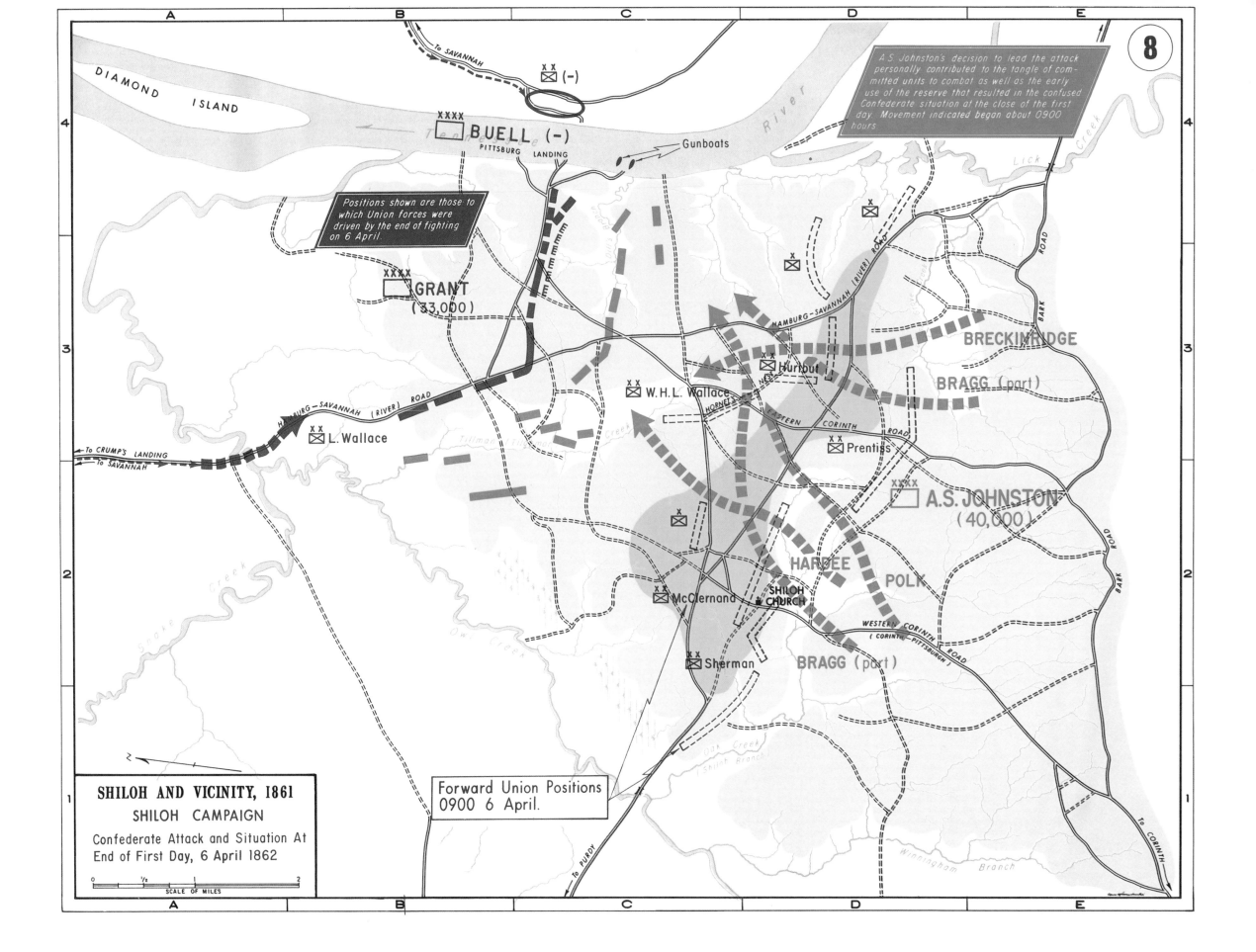

8

A.S. Johnston's decision to lead the attack personally contributed to the tangle of committed units to combat as well as the early use of the reserve that resulted in the confused Confederate situation at the close of the first day. Movement indicated began about 0900 hours.

Positions shown are those to which Union forces were driven by the end of fighting on 6 April.

DIAMOND ISLAND

XX (-)

XXXX BUELL (-)
PITTSBURG LANDING

Gunboats

XXXX GRANT (33,000)

To SAVANNAH

River

Lick Creek

BRECKINRIDGE

BRAGG (part)

XX Hurlbut

XX W.H.L. Wallace

HORNET'S NEST

XX Prentiss

XXXX A.S. JOHNSTON (40,000)

XX L. Wallace

To CRUMP'S LANDING
To SAVANNAH

HARDEE

POLK

XX McClernand

SHILOH CHURCH

WESTERN CORINTH ROAD (CORINTH-PITTSBURGH)

XX Sherman

BRAGG (part)

HAMBURG-SAVANNAH (RIVER) ROAD

EASTERN CORINTH ROAD

BARK ROAD

Forward Union Positions 0900 6 April.

To PURDY

To CORINTH

SHILOH AND VICINITY, 1861
SHILOH CAMPAIGN
Confederate Attack and Situation At
End of First Day, 6 April 1862

0   1/2   1   2
SCALE OF MILES

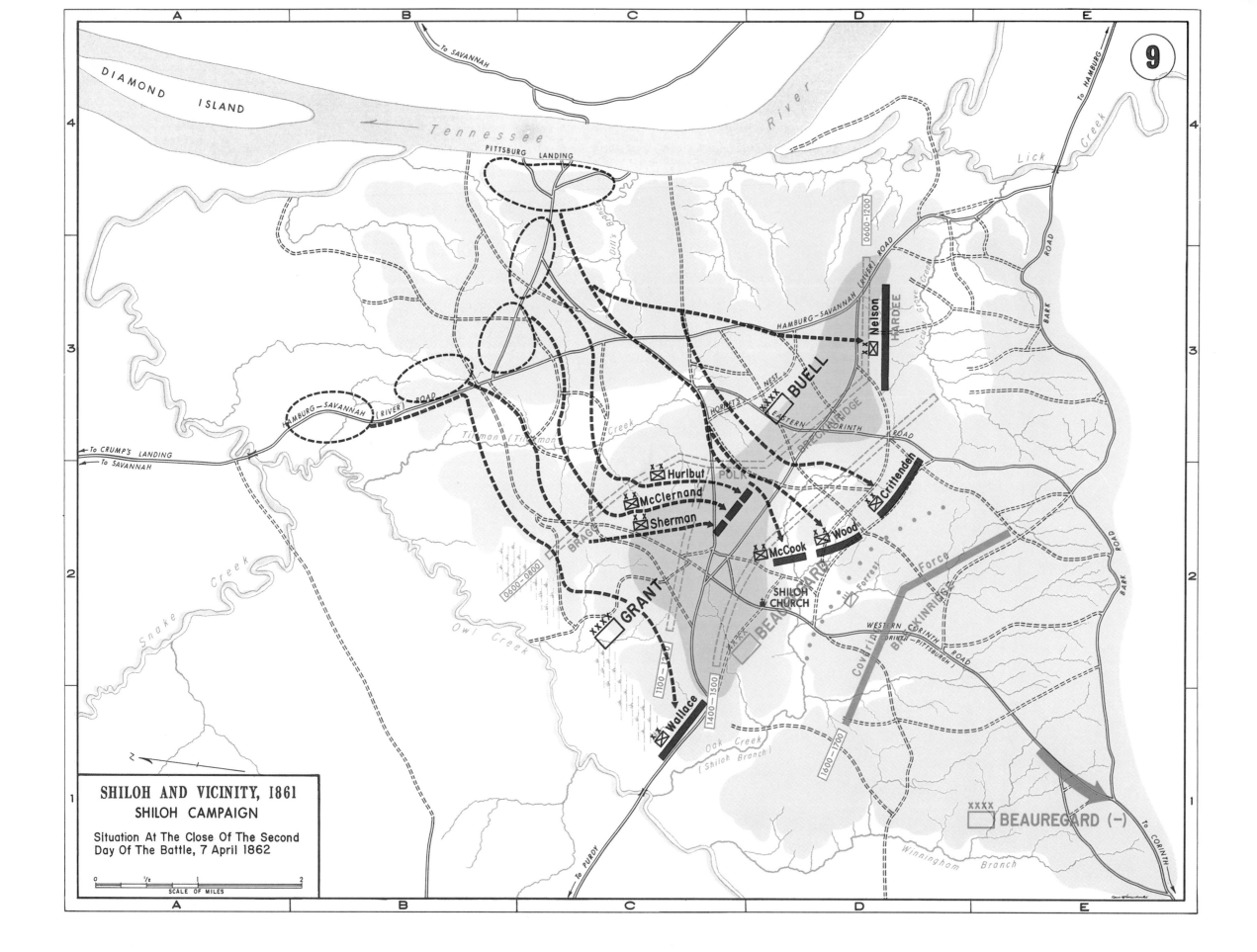

SHILOH AND VICINITY, 1861
SHILOH CAMPAIGN

Situation At The Close Of The Second
Day Of The Battle, 7 April 1862

SCALE OF MILES
0   ½   1   2

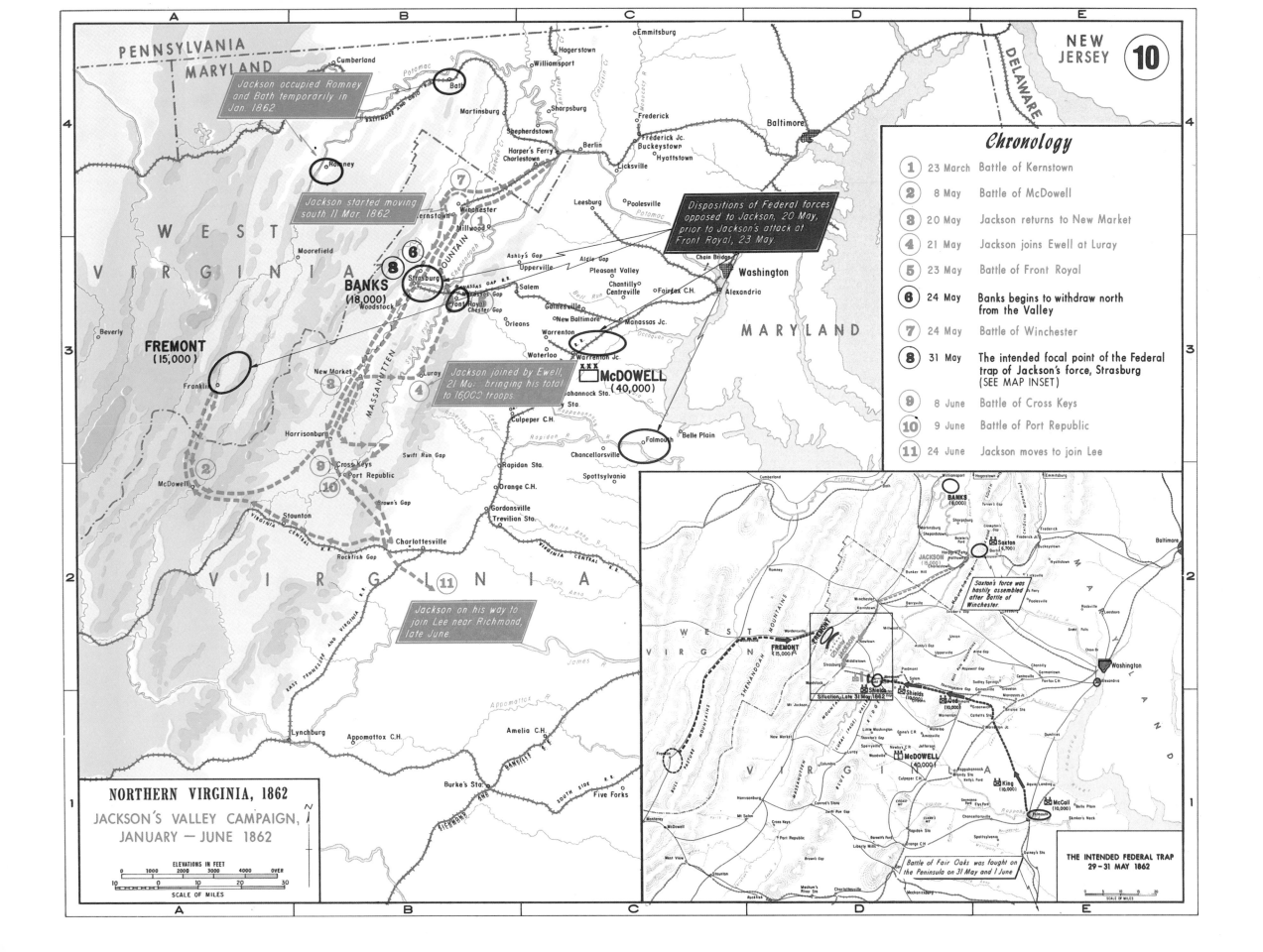

NEW JERSEY

10

Chronology

1	23 March	Battle of Kernstown
2	8 May	Battle of McDowell
3	20 May	Jackson returns to New Market
4	21 May	Jackson joins Ewell at Luray
5	23 May	Battle of Front Royal
6	24 May	Banks begins to withdraw north from the Valley
7	24 May	Battle of Winchester
8	31 May	The intended focal point of the Federal trap of Jackson's force, Strasburg (SEE MAP INSET)
9	8 June	Battle of Cross Keys
10	9 June	Battle of Port Republic
11	24 June	Jackson moves to join Lee

Jackson occupied Romney and Bath temporarily in Jan. 1862

Jackson started moving south 11 Mar. 1862

BANKS (18,000)

FREMONT (15,000)

Dispositions of Federal forces opposed to Jackson, 20 May, prior to Jackson's attack at Front Royal, 23 May.

Jackson joined by Ewell, 21 May, bringing his total to 16,000 troops.

XXX McDOWELL (40,000)

Jackson on his way to join Lee near Richmond, late June.

WEST VIRGINIA

VIRGINIA

MARYLAND

PENNSYLVANIA
MARYLAND

DELAWARE

NORTHERN VIRGINIA, 1862
JACKSON'S VALLEY CAMPAIGN, JANUARY — JUNE 1862

ELEVATIONS IN FEET
0   1000   2000   3000   4000   OVER
10   0   10   20   30
SCALE OF MILES

Saxton's force was hastily assembled after Battle of Winchester

Situation, Late 31 May 1862

Battle of Fair Oaks was fought on the Peninsula on 31 May and 1 June

THE INTENDED FEDERAL TRAP
29 – 31 MAY 1862

SCALE OF MILES

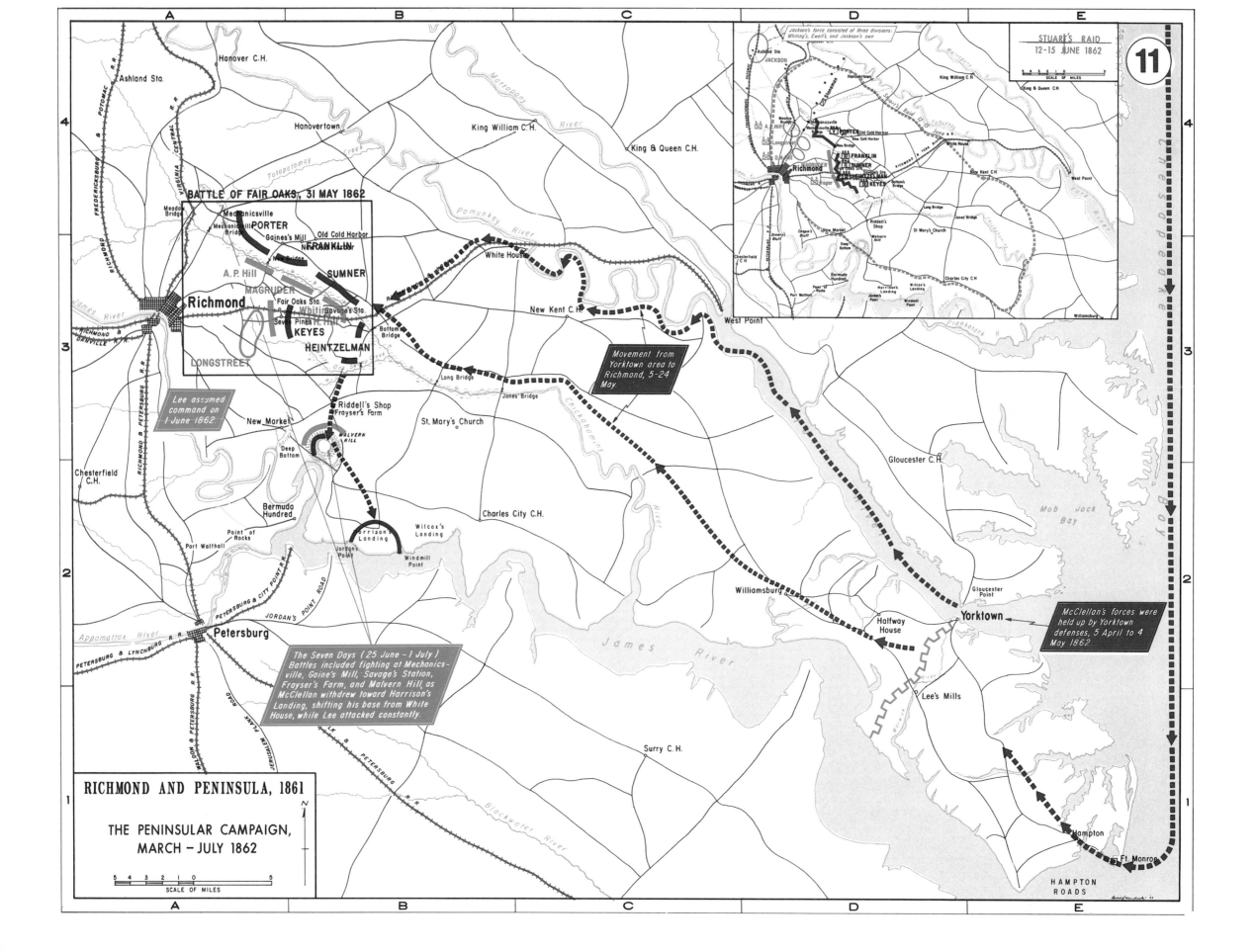

Map labels:

Inset (top right): STUART'S RAID 12-15 JUNE 1862
SCALE OF MILES
Jackson's force consisted of three divisions: Whiting's, Ewell's, and Jackson's own
JACKSON
Ashland Sta.
Hanovertown
King William C.H.
King & Queen C.H.
Stuarts
A.P. Hill
Longstreet
PORTER
Old Cold Harbor
New Cold Harbor
White House
D.H. Hill
FRANKLIN
SUMNER
Richmond
HEINTZELMAN
KEYES
Huger
New Kent C.H.
Long Bridge
Chapin's
Drewry's Bluff
New Market
Riddell's Shop
St Mary's Church
Malvern Hill
Jones Bridge
West Point
New Kent C.H.
Chesterfield C.H.
Bermuda Hundred
Point of Rocks
Port Walthall
Harrison's Landing
Jordan's Point
Windmill Point
Wilcox's Landing
Deep Bottom
Charles City C.H.
Williamsburg

(11)

Main map:

A.4 B.4 C.4 D.4 E.4
Ashland Sta.
Hanover C.H.
Hanovertown
King William C.H.
King & Queen C.H.
Meadow Bridge
Mechanicsville
Mechanicsville Bridge
PORTER
Gaines's Mill
Old Cold Harbor
New Bridge
FRANKLIN
SUMNER
A.P. Hill
MAGRUDER
Richmond
Fair Oaks Sta.
Savage's Sta.
Whiting
Seven Pines
D.H. Hill
KEYES
HEINTZELMAN
BATTLE OF FAIR OAKS, 31 MAY 1862
LONGSTREET
Bottom Bridge
White House
New Kent C.H.
West Point
Pamunkey River
Mattapony River

Lee assumed command on 1 June 1862
New Market
Riddell's Shop
Frayser's Farm
St. Mary's Church
Long Bridge
Jones' Bridge
Chickahominy River

Movement from Yorktown area to Richmond, 5-24 May.

Chesterfield C.H.
Bermuda Hundred
Point of Rocks
Port Walthall
Jordan's Point
Deep Bottom
Malvern Hill
Harrison's Landing
Wilcox's Landing
Windmill Point
Charles City C.H.
Gloucester C.H.
Mob Jack Bay

Petersburg
Appomattox River

The Seven Days (25 June - 1 July) Battles included fighting at Mechanicsville, Gaine's Mill, Savage's Station, Frayser's Farm, and Malvern Hill, as McClellan withdrew toward Harrison's Landing, shifting his base from White House, while Lee attacked constantly.

James River
Williamsburg
Halfway House
Yorktown
Gloucester Point
Lee's Mills

McClellan's forces were held up by Yorktown defenses, 5 April to 4 May 1862

Surry C.H.
Blackwater River

Hampton
Ft. Monroe
HAMPTON ROADS

RICHMOND AND PENINSULA, 1861
THE PENINSULAR CAMPAIGN, MARCH - JULY 1862

N
5 4 3 2 1 0   5
SCALE OF MILES

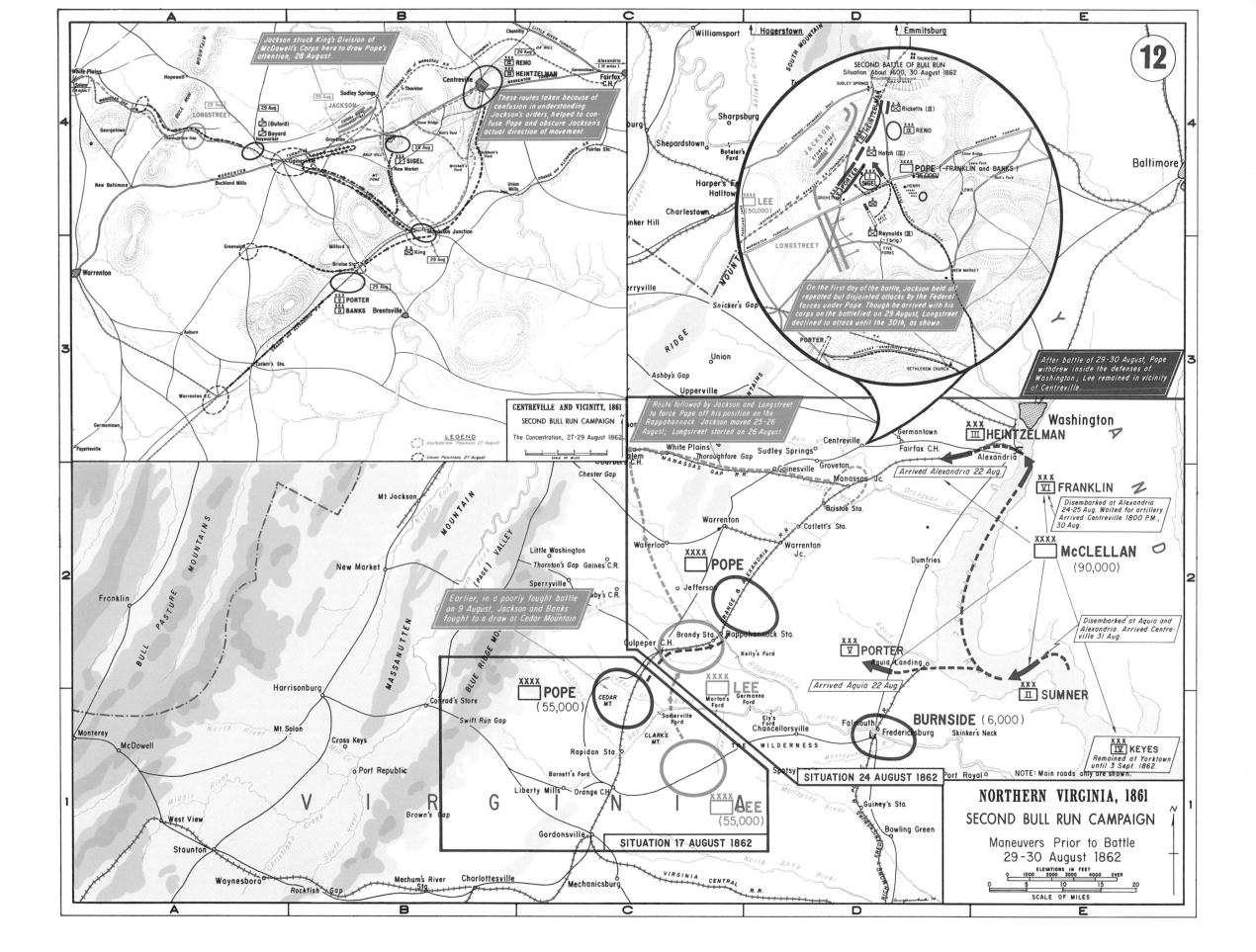

Upper left inset — "Centreville and Vicinity, 1861":

Jackson struck King's Division of McDowell's Corps here to draw Pope's attention, 28 August.

These routes taken because of confusion in understanding Jackson's orders, helped to confuse Pope and obscure Jackson's actual direction of movement.

RENO
HEINTZELMAN

Centreville

Fairfax C.H.

Alexandria (15 miles)

LONGSTREET

JACKSON

SIGEL

Gainesville

BALD HILL

New Market

King

PORTER
BANKS

Brentsville

Warrenton

Manassas Junction

CENTREVILLE AND VICINITY, 1861
SECOND BULL RUN CAMPAIGN
The Concentration, 27-29 August 1862

LEGEND
Confederate Positions 27 August
Union Positions 27 August

SCALE OF MILES

Upper right inset (circle 12) — "Second Battle of Bull Run":

SECOND BATTLE OF BULL RUN
Situation About 1600, 30 August 1862

SCALE OF MILES

Ricketts (III)
RENO
Hatch (III)
JACKSON
THORNTON
SUDLEY SPRINGS
POPE (Franklin and Banks)
PORTER
SIGEL
LEE (50,000)
LONGSTREET
Reynolds (I brig.)
FIVE FORKS
NEW MARKET

On the first day of the battle, Jackson held off repeated but disjointed attacks by the Federal forces under Pope. Though he arrived with his corps on the battlefield on 29 August, Longstreet declined to attack until the 30th, as shown.

After battle of 29-30 August, Pope withdrew inside the defenses of Washington; Lee remained in vicinity of Centreville.

Main map:

Williamsport — Hagerstown — Emmitsburg

SOUTH MOUNTAIN

Sharpsburg
Shepardstown
Harper's Ferry
Halltown
Charlestown
Bunker Hill
Snicker's Gap
Ashby's Gap
Upperville
Union
RIDGE
MOUNTAINS

Baltimore

Route followed by Jackson and Longstreet to force Pope off his position on the Rappahannock. Jackson moved 25-26 August; Longstreet started on 26 August.

Germantown
Centreville
Fairfax C.H.
Alexandria
Sudley Springs
White Plains
Thoroughfare Gap
Gainesville
Groveton
Manassas Jc.
Bristoe Sta.
Warrenton
Waterloo
Catlett's Sta.
Warrenton Jc.
Dumfries

Washington
HEINTZELMAN

Arrived Alexandria 22 Aug.

FRANKLIN
Disembarked at Alexandria 24-25 Aug. Waited for artillery. Arrived Centreville 1800 P.M., 30 Aug.

McCLELLAN (90,000)

POPE

Earlier, in a poorly fought battle on 9 August, Jackson and Banks fought to a draw at Cedar Mountain

Jefferson
Brandy Sta.
Rappahannock Sta.
Kelly's Ford
Culpeper C.H.
CEDAR MT.
POPE (55,000)
Somerville Ford
CLARK'S MT.
Rapidan Sta.
Barnett's Ford
Liberty Mills
Orange C.H.
Morton's Ford
Germanna Ford
Ely's Ford
Chancellorsville
THE WILDERNESS

LEE

PORTER
Aquia Landing
Arrived Aquia 22 Aug.

SUMNER

BURNSIDE (6,000)
Falmouth
Fredericksburg
Skinker's Neck

Disembarked at Aquia and Alexandria. Arrived Centreville 31 Aug.

KEYES
Remained at Yorktown until 3 Sept. 1862.

SITUATION 24 AUGUST 1862

Franklin
Mt. Jackson
New Market
Little Washington
Thornton's Gap
Gaines C.R.
Sperryville

BULL PASTURE MOUNTAINS
MASSANUTTEN MOUNTAIN
BLUE RIDGE MOUNTAINS
(PAGE) VALLEY

Harrisonburg
Conrad's Store
Swift Run Gap
Mt. Solon
Cross Keys
Monterey
McDowell
Port Republic
West View
Staunton
Waynesboro
Rockfish Gap
Mechum's River Sta.
Charlottesville
Mechanicsburg

POPE (55,000)
CEDAR MT.

LEE (55,000)
Gordonsville

SITUATION 17 AUGUST 1862

V I R G I N I A

Guiney's Sta.
Bowling Green
Port Royal

NOTE: Main roads only are shown.

NORTHERN VIRGINIA, 1861
SECOND BULL RUN CAMPAIGN
Maneuvers Prior to Battle
29-30 August 1862

ELEVATIONS IN FEET
1000 2000 3000 4000 OVER

SCALE OF MILES
0 5 10 15 20

N

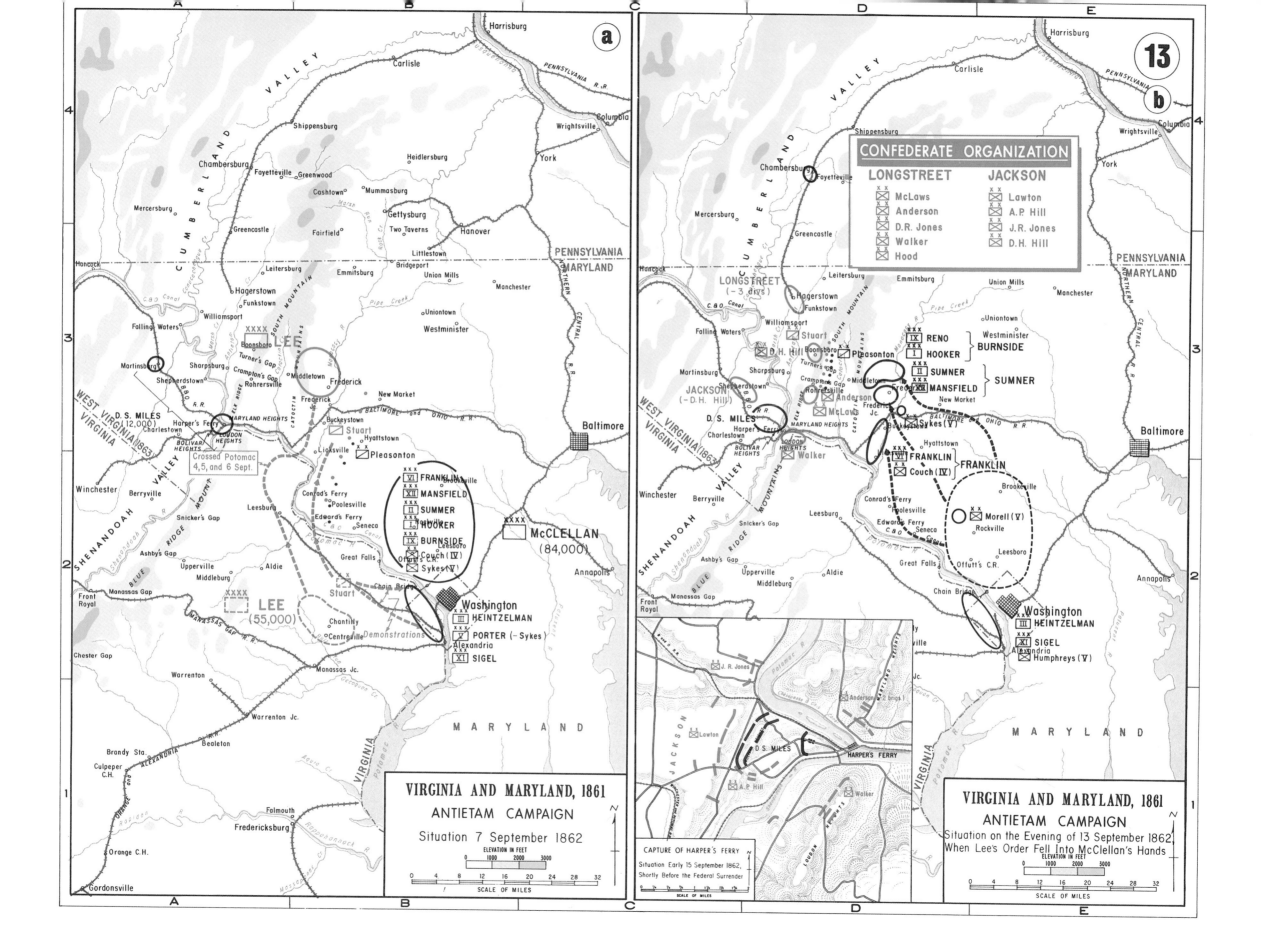

a

13

b

CONFEDERATE ORGANIZATION

LONGSTREET	JACKSON
McLaws	Lawton
Anderson	A.P. Hill
D.R. Jones	J.R. Jones
Walker	D.H. Hill
Hood	

Map a (left):

LEE

D.S. MILES (12,000)

Crossed Potomac 4,5, and 6 Sept.

Stuart

Pleasonton

VI FRANKLIN
XII MANSFIELD
II SUMMER
I HOOKER
IX BURNSIDE
Couch (IV)
Sykes (V)

McCLELLAN (84,000)

LEE (55,000)

Stuart

Demonstrations

Washington
III HEINTZELMAN
V PORTER (- Sykes)
Alexandria
XI SIGEL

VIRGINIA AND MARYLAND, 1861
ANTIETAM CAMPAIGN
Situation 7 September 1862

ELEVATION IN FEET
0 1000 2000 3000
0 4 8 12 16 20 24 28 32
SCALE OF MILES

Map b (right):

LONGSTREET (- 3 divs)

Stuart

D.H. Hill

Pleasonton

IX RENO
I HOOKER BURNSIDE
II SUMNER
XII MANSFIELD SUMNER

JACKSON (- D.H. Hill)

D.S. MILES

Anderson

McLaws

Sykes (V)

Walker

VI FRANKLIN
Couch (IV) FRANKLIN

Morell (V)

Rockville

Offutt's C.R.

Washington
III HEINTZELMAN
XI SIGEL
Alexandria
Humphreys (V)

VIRGINIA AND MARYLAND, 1861
ANTIETAM CAMPAIGN
Situation on the Evening of 13 September 1862,
When Lee's Order Fell Into McClellan's Hands

ELEVATION IN FEET
0 1000 2000 3000
0 4 8 12 16 20 24 28 32
SCALE OF MILES

Inset (Capture of Harper's Ferry):

J.R. Jones

Anderson (2 brigs.)

JACKSON

Lawton

D.S. MILES

HARPER'S FERRY

A.P. Hill

Walker

CAPTURE OF HARPER'S FERRY
Situation Early 15 September 1862,
Shortly Before the Federal Surrender

SCALE OF MILES

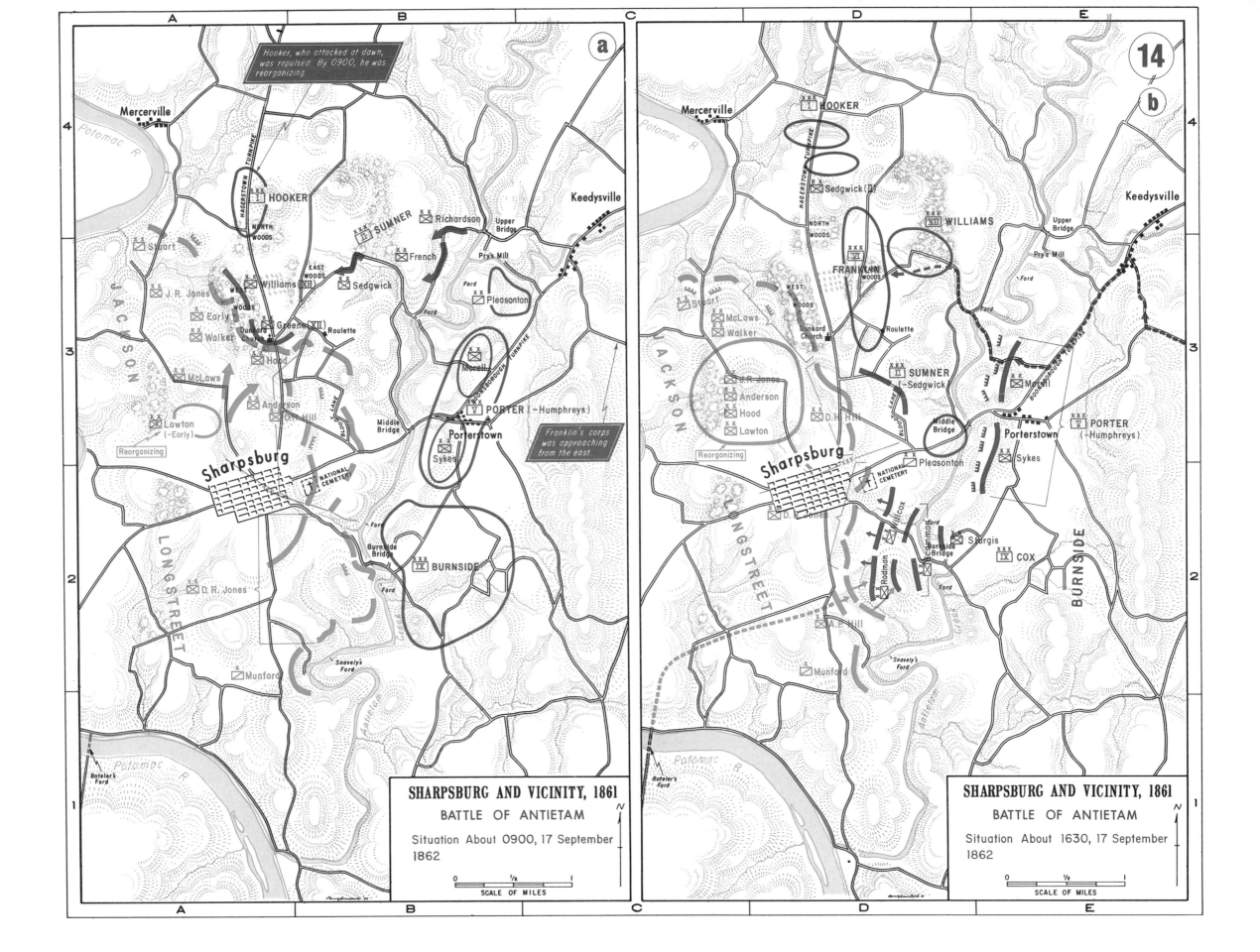

Map a labels:

Mercerville · Potomac R. · HOOKER · Hagerstown Turnpike · NORTH WOODS · SUMNER · Richardson · Upper Bridge · Keedysville · Stuart · Williams · EAST WOODS · French · Pry's Mill · Ford · J.R. Jones · Sedgwick · Ford · Early · Greene · Roulette · Pleasonton · Walker · Dunkard Church · Hood · McLaws · Anderson · D.H. Hill · Bloody Lane · Morell · Lawton (-Early) · Reorganizing · Middle Bridge · PORTER (-Humphreys) · JACKSON · Porterstown · Boonsborough Turnpike · Sharpsburg · NATIONAL CEMETERY · Sykes · Ford · Franklin's corps was approaching from the east. · LONGSTREET · Burnside Bridge · Ford · BURNSIDE · D.R. Jones · Antietam · Munford · Snavely's Ford · Bateler's Ford · Potomac R.

Hooker, who attacked at dawn, was repulsed. By 0900, he was reorganizing.

SHARPSBURG AND VICINITY, 1861
BATTLE OF ANTIETAM
Situation About 0900, 17 September 1862
0   1/2   1
SCALE OF MILES
N

Map b labels:

a
14
b

Mercerville · Potomac R. · HOOKER · Hagerstown Turnpike · Sedgwick (II) · NORTH WOODS · WILLIAMS · Upper Bridge · Pry's Mill · Keedysville · FRANKLIN · WEST WOODS · Stuart · McLaws · Walker · Dunkard Church · Roulette · Ford · SUMNER (-Sedgwick) · JACKSON · D.R. Jones · Anderson · D.H. Hill · Bloody Lane · Morell · Hood · Lawton · Middle Bridge · PORTER (-Humphreys) · Reorganizing · Sharpsburg · NATIONAL CEMETERY · Pleasonton · Porterstown · Boonsborough Turnpike · Sykes · D.R. Jones · Willcox · Ford · Sturgis · Rodman · Burnside Bridge · COX · LONGSTREET · Antietam · Ford · BURNSIDE · A.P. Hill · Munford · Snavely's Ford · Bateler's Ford · Potomac R.

SHARPSBURG AND VICINITY, 1861
BATTLE OF ANTIETAM
Situation About 1630, 17 September 1862
0   1/2   1
SCALE OF MILES
N

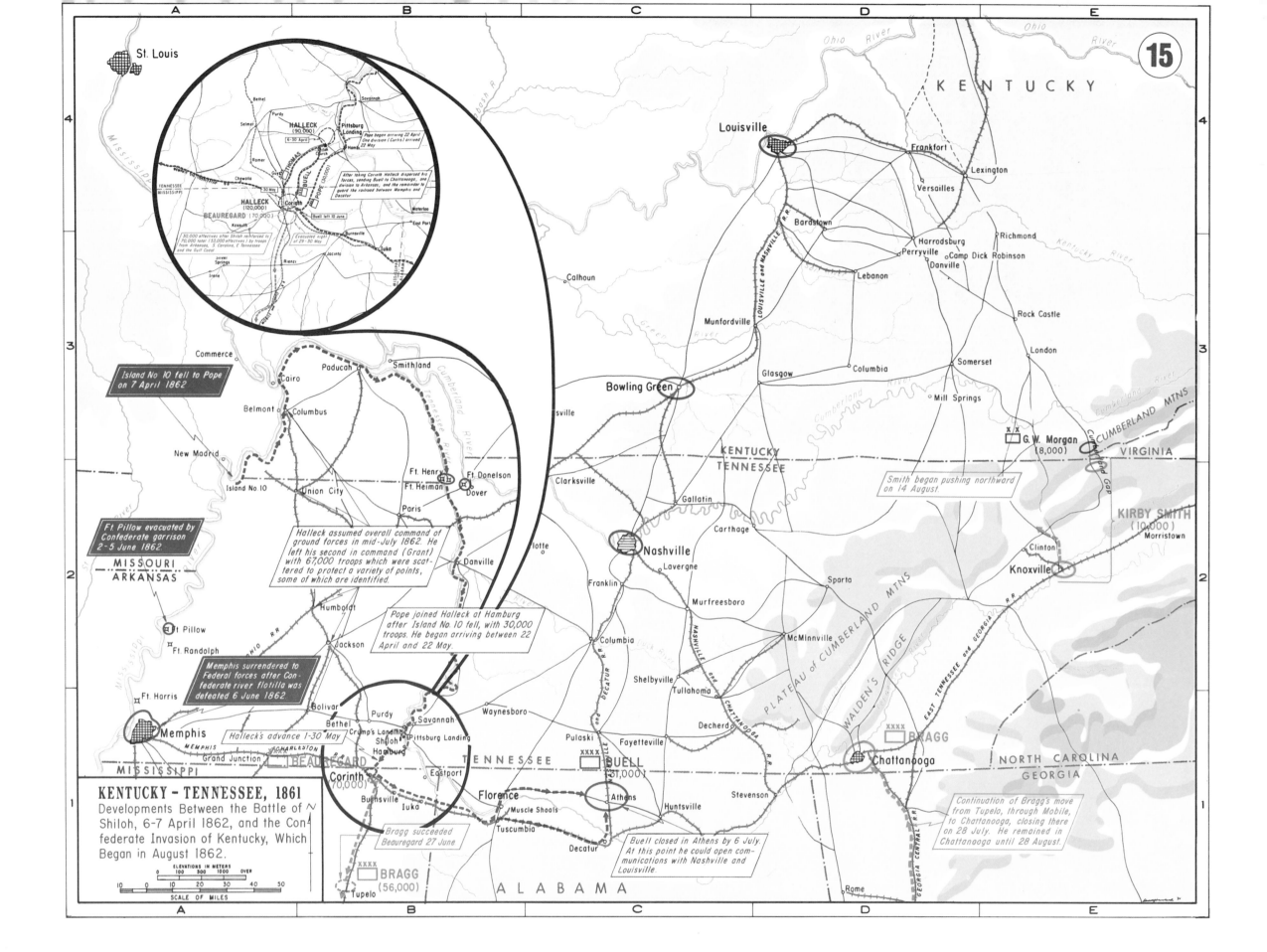

Map label 15 (top right)

KENTUCKY — TENNESSEE, 1861
Developments Between the Battle of
Shiloh, 6-7 April 1862, and the Con-
federate Invasion of Kentucky, Which
Began in August 1862.

ELEVATIONS IN METERS
100 500 1000 OVER
SCALE OF MILES
10   0   10   20   30   40   50

Island No. 10 fell to Pope
on 7 April 1862.

Ft. Pillow evacuated by
Confederate garrison
2-5 June 1862.

Memphis surrendered to Federal forces after Confederate river flotilla was defeated 6 June 1862.

Halleck assumed overall command of
ground forces in mid-July 1862. He
left his second in command (Grant)
with 67,000 troops which were scat-
tered to protect a variety of points,
some of which are identified.

Pope joined Halleck at Hamburg
after Island No. 10 fell, with 30,000
troops. He began arriving between 22
April and 22 May.

Halleck's advance 1-30 May

Bragg succeeded Beauregard 27 June

Smith began pushing northward
on 14 August.

Buell closed in Athens by 6 July.
At this point he could open com-
munications with Nashville and
Louisville.

Continuation of Bragg's move
from Tupelo, through Mobile,
to Chattanooga, closing there
on 28 July. He remained in
Chattanooga until 28 August.

Inset (upper left):

HALLECK (90,000)
6-30 April
Pope arriving 22 April
One division (Curtis) arrived
22 May
After taking Corinth Halleck dispersed his
forces, sending Buell to Chattanooga, one
division to Arkansas, and the remainder to
guard the railroad between Memphis and
Decatur.
THOMAS
BUELL (30,000)
POPE
HALLECK (120,000)
BEAUREGARD (70,000)
Buell left 10 June.
Evacuated night
of 29-30 May
30,000 effectives after Shiloh reinforced to
70,000 total (53,000 effectives) by troops
from Arkansas, S. Carolina, E. Tennessee
and the Gulf Coast

Unit labels:
G. W. Morgan (8,000)
KIRBY SMITH (10,000)
BRAGG
BUELL (31,000)
BEAUREGARD
Corinth (70,000)
BRAGG (56,000)

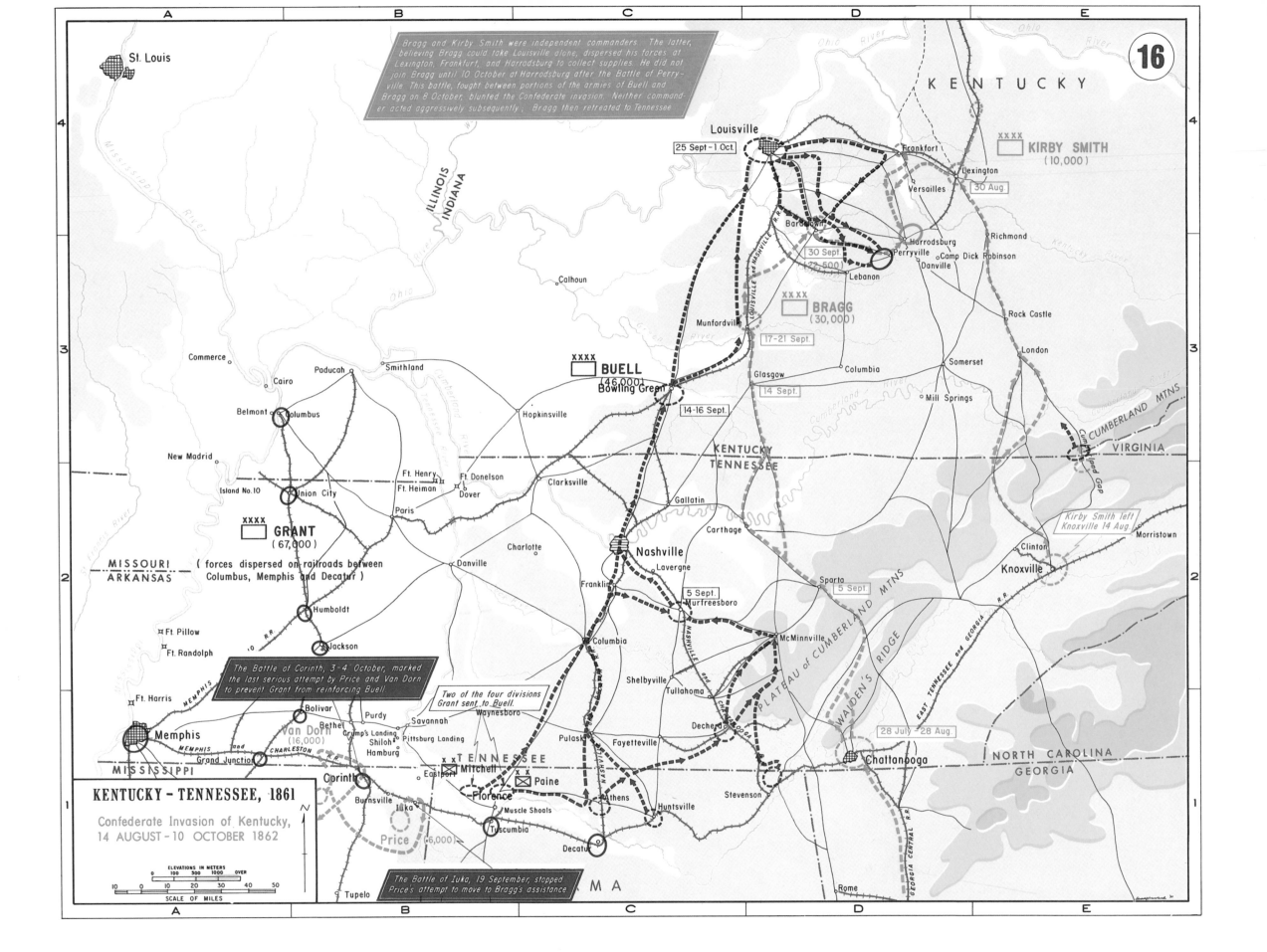

16

Bragg and Kirby Smith were independent commanders. The latter, believing Bragg could take Louisville alone, dispersed his forces at Lexington, Frankfort, and Harrodsburg to collect supplies. He did not join Bragg until 10 October at Harrodsburg after the Battle of Perryville. This battle, fought between portions of the armies of Buell and Bragg on 8 October, blunted the Confederate invasion. Neither commander acted aggressively subsequently; Bragg then retreated to Tennessee.

KENTUCKY

St. Louis

ILLINOIS
INDIANA

XXXX KIRBY SMITH
(10,000)

Louisville
25 Sept–1 Oct.

Frankfort
Lexington
30 Aug.
Versailles

Bardstown
Harrodsburg
Richmond
30 Sept.
(27,500)
Perryville
Camp Dick Robinson
Danville
Lebanon

Calhoun

XXXX BRAGG
(30,000)

Rock Castle

Munfordville
17–21 Sept.
London

Commerce
Cairo
Paducah
Smithland

Belmont
Columbus

XXXX BUELL
(46,000)
Bowling Green
14–16 Sept.

Glasgow
14 Sept.
Columbia
Somerset

Hopkinsville

Mill Springs

KENTUCKY
TENNESSEE

New Madrid

Island No.10
Union City

Ft. Henry
Ft. Heiman
Ft. Donelson
Dover

Clarksville

Gallatin

CUMBERLAND MTNS
VIRGINIA

Paris

Cumberland Gap

Kirby Smith left
Knoxville 14 Aug.
Morristown

XXXX GRANT
(67,000)

(forces dispersed on railroads between
Columbus, Memphis and Decatur)

MISSOURI
ARKANSAS

Charlotte
Danville

Nashville
Lavergne

Carthage

Sparta
5 Sept.

Clinton
Knoxville

Humboldt

Franklin

5 Sept.
Murfreesboro

Ft. Pillow
Ft. Randolph
Jackson

Columbia

McMinnville

PLATEAU of CUMBERLAND MTNS
WALDEN'S RIDGE

The Battle of Corinth, 3–4 October, marked
the last serious attempt by Price and Van Dorn
to prevent Grant from reinforcing Buell.

Shelbyville
Tullahoma

Ft. Harris

Bolivar
Bethel
Purdy
Grump's Landing
Savannah
Pittsburg Landing
Hamburg

Two of the four divisions
Grant sent to Buell.

Waynesboro

Pulaski
Fayetteville

Decherd

28 July – 28 Aug.

EAST TENNESSEE and GEORGIA R.R.

NORTH CAROLINA
GEORGIA

Memphis

Grand Junction

Van Dorn
(16,000)

Shiloh

x x TENNESSEE
Mitchell
x x Paine

Athens
Huntsville

Stevenson
Chattanooga

MISSISSIPPI

Corinth
Burnsville
Iuka

Florence

Muscle Shoals
Tuscumbia
Decatur

GEORGIA CENTRAL R.R.

KENTUCKY – TENNESSEE, 1861

Confederate Invasion of Kentucky,
14 AUGUST – 10 OCTOBER 1862

N

Price (6,000)

A M A

The Battle of Iuka, 19 September, stopped
Price's attempt to move to Bragg's assistance

Rome

ELEVATIONS IN METERS
100 300 1000 OVER

SCALE OF MILES

Tupelo

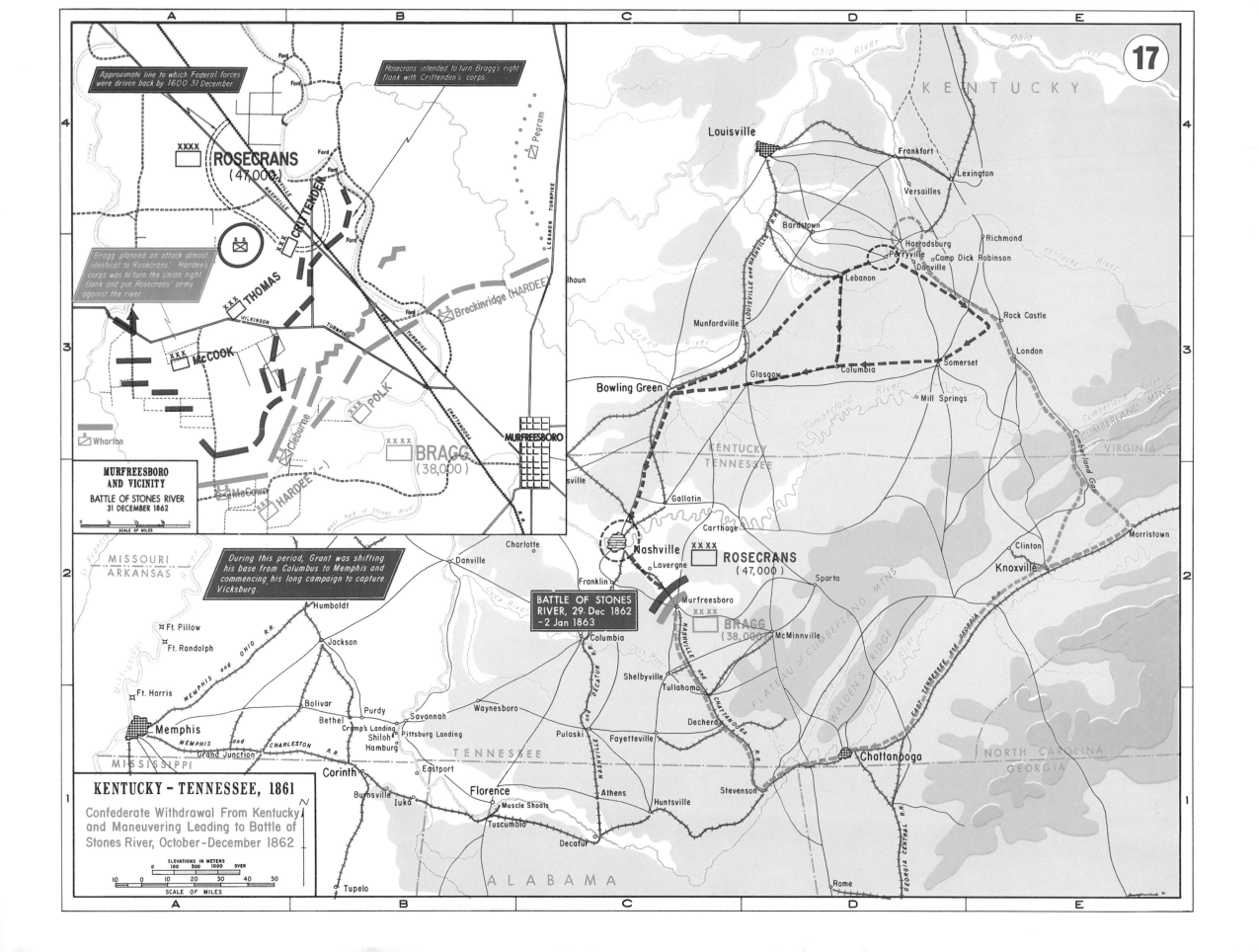

Inset map — upper left (Murfreesboro and Vicinity):

Approximate line to which Federal forces were driven back by 1600 31 December

Rosecrans intended to turn Bragg's right flank with Crittenden's corps.

XXXX ROSECRANS (47,000)

CRITTENDEN

Bragg planned an attack almost identical to Rosecrans'. Hardee's corps was to turn the Union right flank and pin Rosecrans' army against the river.

XXX THOMAS

XXX WILKINSON

XXX McCOOK

Wharton

POLK

Cleburne

McCOWN

HARDEE

Breckinridge (HARDEE)

Pegram

LEBANON TURNPIKE

NASHVILLE

TURNPIKE

CHATTANOOGA R.R.

MURFREESBORO

XXXX BRAGG (38,000)

MURFREESBORO AND VICINITY

BATTLE OF STONES RIVER 31 DECEMBER 1862

SCALE OF MILES

Main map:

KENTUCKY

Ohio River

Louisville

Frankfort

Lexington

Versailles

Bardstown

Harrodsburg

Richmond

Perryville

Camp Dick Robinson

Danville

Lebanon

Kentucky River

LOUISVILLE AND NASHVILLE R.R.

Munfordville

Rock Castle

Salt River

Green River

Mill Springs

Columbia

Somerset

London

Glasgow

Bowling Green

Cumberland River

CUMBERLAND MTNS

KENTUCKY

TENNESSEE

VIRGINIA

Cumberland Gap

lhoun

Gallatin

Carthage

Duck River

Nashville

Lavergne

Morristown

Clinton

Knoxville

XXXX ROSECRANS (47,000)

Franklin

Murfreesboro

Sparta

BATTLE OF STONES RIVER, 29 Dec 1862 - 2 Jan 1863

XXXX BRAGG (38,000)

McMinnville

Columbia

R.R.

Duck River

Shelbyville

Tullahoma

Plateau of Cumberland Mtns

WALDEN'S RIDGE

Tennessee River

EAST TENNESSEE AND GEORGIA R.R.

NASHVILLE and DECATUR R.R.

Pulaski

Fayetteville

Decherd

NASHVILLE and CHATTANOOGA R.R.

Stevenson

Chattanooga

NORTH CAROLINA

GEORGIA

During this period, Grant was shifting his base from Columbus to Memphis and commencing his long campaign to capture Vicksburg.

MISSOURI

ARKANSAS

St. Francis River

Charlotte

Danville

Humboldt

MEMPHIS AND OHIO R.R.

Ft. Pillow

Ft. Randolph

Jackson

Ft. Harris

Bolivar

Purdy

Bethel

Cramp's Landing

Savannah

Waynesboro

Shiloh

Pittsburg Landing

Hamburg

Memphis

MEMPHIS and CHARLESTON R.R.

Grand Junction

MISSISSIPPI

Corinth

TENNESSEE

Eastport

Athens

Huntsville

ALABAMA

Burnsville

Iuka

Florence

Muscle Shoals

Tuscumbia

Decatur

Rome

GEORGIA CENTRAL R.R.

Tupelo

KENTUCKY - TENNESSEE, 1861

Confederate Withdrawal From Kentucky and Maneuvering Leading to Battle of Stones River, October-December 1862

ELEVATIONS IN METERS
100 500 1000 OVER

SCALE OF MILES

17

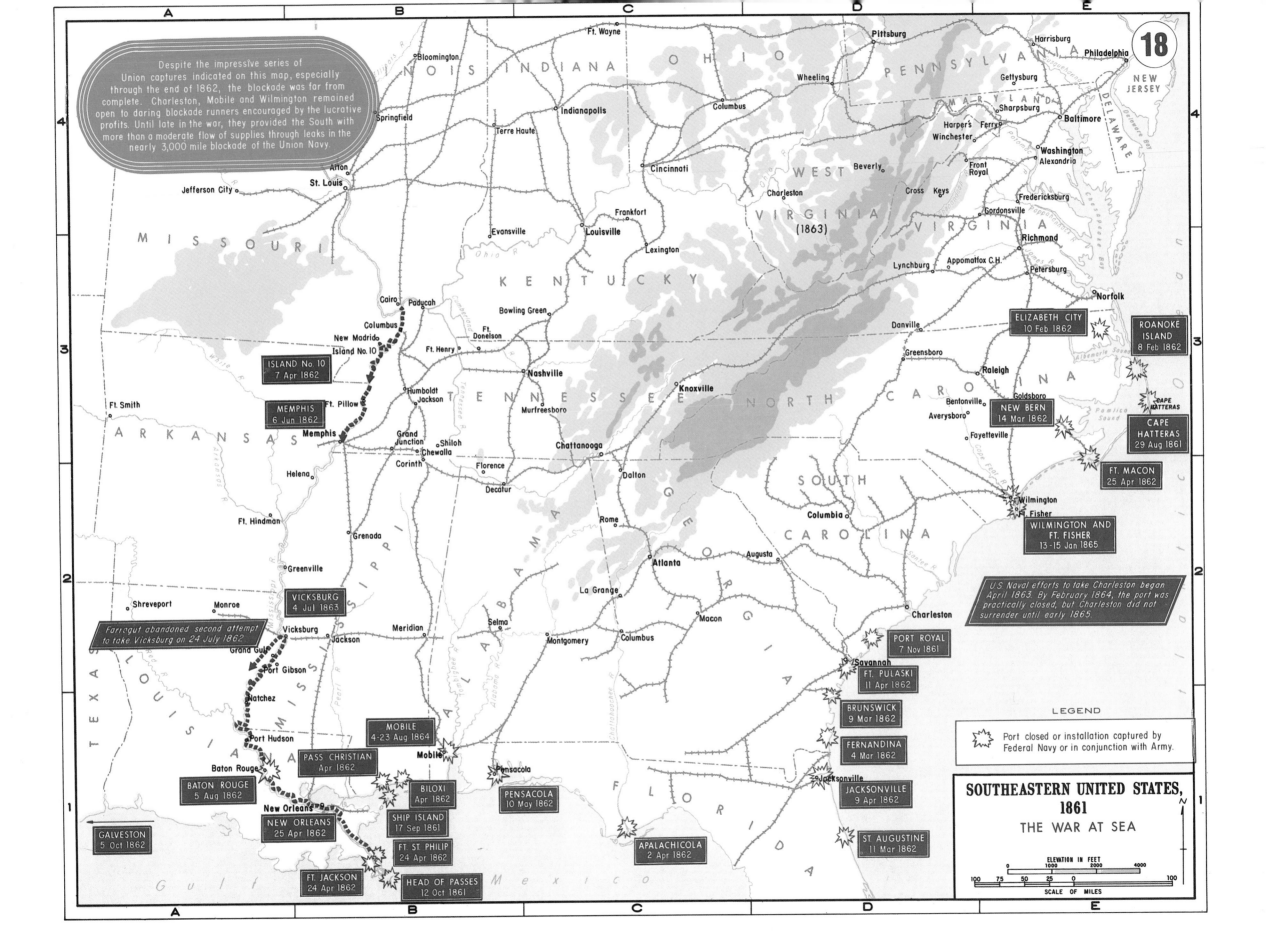

Despite the impressive series of Union captures indicated on this map, especially through the end of 1862, the blockade was far from complete. Charleston, Mobile and Wilmington remained open to daring blockade runners encouraged by the lucrative profits. Until late in the war, they provided the South with more than a moderate flow of supplies through leaks in the nearly 3,000 mile blockade of the Union Navy.

U.S. Naval efforts to take Charleston began April 1863. By February 1864, the port was practically closed, but Charleston did not surrender until early 1865.

Farragut abandoned second attempt to take Vicksburg on 24 July 1862.

ISLAND No. 10
7 Apr 1862

MEMPHIS
6 Jun 1862

VICKSBURG
4 Jul 1863

BATON ROUGE
5 Aug 1862

PASS CHRISTIAN
Apr 1862

MOBILE
4-23 Aug 1864

NEW ORLEANS
25 Apr 1862

GALVESTON
5 Oct 1862

BILOXI
Apr 1862

SHIP ISLAND
17 Sep 1861

FT. ST. PHILIP
24 Apr 1862

FT. JACKSON
24 Apr 1862

HEAD OF PASSES
12 Oct 1861

PENSACOLA
10 May 1862

APALACHICOLA
2 Apr 1862

ST. AUGUSTINE
11 Mar 1862

JACKSONVILLE
9 Apr 1862

FERNANDINA
4 Mar 1862

BRUNSWICK
9 Mar 1862

FT. PULASKI
11 Apr 1862

PORT ROYAL
7 Nov 1861

ELIZABETH CITY
10 Feb 1862

ROANOKE ISLAND
8 Feb 1862

NEW BERN
14 Mar 1862

CAPE HATTERAS
29 Aug 1861

FT. MACON
25 Apr 1862

WILMINGTON AND FT. FISHER
13-15 Jan 1865

LEGEND

Port closed or installation captured by Federal Navy or in conjunction with Army.

SOUTHEASTERN UNITED STATES, 1861
THE WAR AT SEA

ELEVATION IN FEET
1000   2000   4000

100   75   50   25   0   100
SCALE OF MILES

18

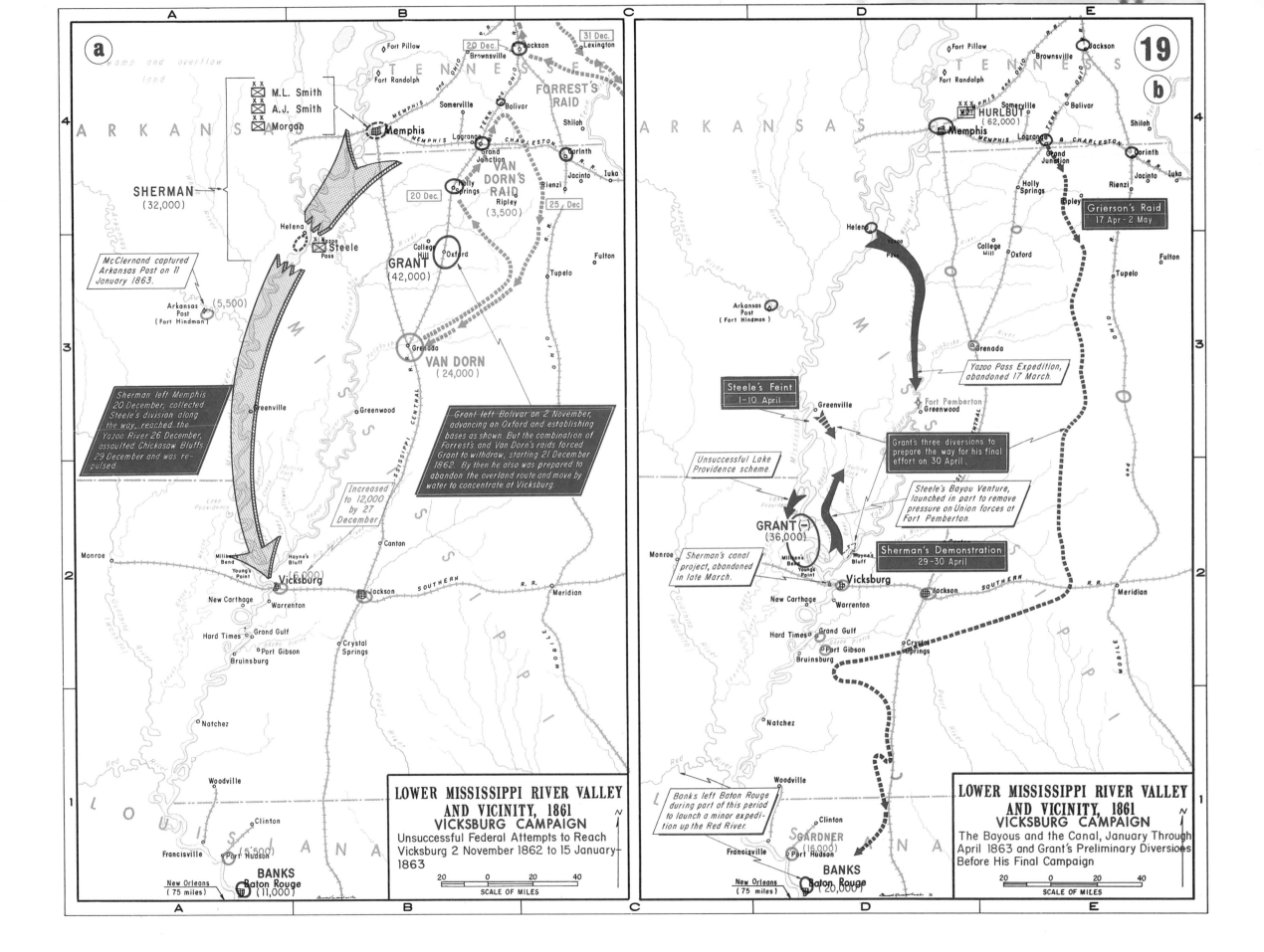

Map (a) — left panel

A — B — C (top column labels); 4, 3, 2, 1 (side row labels)

Swamp and overflow land

TENNESSEE

Fort Pillow
Fort Randolph
Brownsville
Jackson
20 Dec.
31 Dec.
Lexington

XX M.L. Smith
XX A.J. Smith
XX Morgan

Somerville
Bolivar
Shiloh
Memphis
Lagrange
Grand Junction
Charleston
Corinth
Jacinto · Iuka
Rienzi

FORREST'S RAID

ARKANSAS

SHERMAN (32,000)

Holly Springs
20 Dec.
Ripley (3,500)
25 Dec.

VAN DORN'S RAID

Helena
X Yazoo Pass
Steele

College Hill
Oxford

GRANT (42,000)

Fulton

McClernand captured Arkansas Post on 11 January 1863.

(5,500)

Arkansas Post (Fort Hindman)

Grenada

VAN DORN (24,000)

Sherman left Memphis 20 December, collected Steele's division along the way, reached the Yazoo River 26 December, assaulted Chickasaw Bluffs 29 December and was repulsed.

Greenville
Greenwood

Grant left Bolivar on 2 November, advancing on Oxford and establishing bases as shown. But the combination of Forrest's and Van Dorn's raids forced Grant to withdraw, starting 21 December 1862. By then he also was prepared to abandon the overland route and move by water to concentrate at Vicksburg.

Increased to 12,000 by 27 December

Canton

Milliken's Bend
Haynes' Bluff
Young's Point (6,000)
Vicksburg
Jackson
SOUTHERN R.R.
Meridian

Monroe

New Carthage
Warrenton

Hard Times · Grand Gulf
Port Gibson
Bruinsburg
Crystal Springs

Natchez

LOUISIANA

Woodville
Clinton
Francisville
(5,500)
Port Hudson

New Orleans (75 miles)
BANKS Baton Rouge (11,000)

LOWER MISSISSIPPI RIVER VALLEY AND VICINITY, 1861 VICKSBURG CAMPAIGN
Unsuccessful Federal Attempts to Reach Vicksburg 2 November 1862 to 15 January 1863

20 0 20 40
SCALE OF MILES

Map (b) — right panel

19
b

D — E (top column labels); 4, 3, 2, 1 (side row labels)

TENNESSEE

Fort Pillow
Fort Randolph
Brownsville
Jackson
Somerville
Bolivar
Shiloh

XXX **HURLBUT** (62,000)

Memphis
Lagrange
Grand Junction
Charleston
Corinth
Jacinto · Iuka
Rienzi

ARKANSAS

Grierson's Raid 17 Apr - 2 May

Holly Springs
Ripley

Helena
Yazoo Pass

College Hill
Oxford

Fulton
Tupelo

Arkansas Post (Fort Hindman)

Grenada

Yazoo Pass Expedition, abandoned 17 March.

Steele's Feint 1-10 April

Greenville
Fort Pemberton
Greenwood

Grant's three diversions to prepare the way for his final effort on 30 April.

Unsuccessful Lake Providence scheme.

Steele's Bayou Venture, launched in part to remove pressure on Union forces at Fort Pemberton.

GRANT (–) (36,000)

Monroe
Sherman's canal project, abandoned in late March.

Milliken's Bend
Haynes' Bluff
Young's Point

Sherman's Demonstration 29-30 April

Vicksburg
Jackson
SOUTHERN R.R.
Meridian

New Carthage
Warrenton

Hard Times · Grand Gulf
Port Gibson
Bruinsburg
Crystal Springs

Natchez

LOUISIANA

Woodville

Banks left Baton Rouge during part of this period to launch a minor expedition up the Red River.

Clinton
GARDNER (16,000)
Francisville
Port Hudson

New Orleans (75 miles)
BANKS Baton Rouge (20,000)

LOWER MISSISSIPPI RIVER VALLEY AND VICINITY, 1861 VICKSBURG CAMPAIGN
The Bayous and the Canal, January Through April 1863 and Grant's Preliminary Diversions Before His Final Campaign

20 0 20 40
SCALE OF MILES

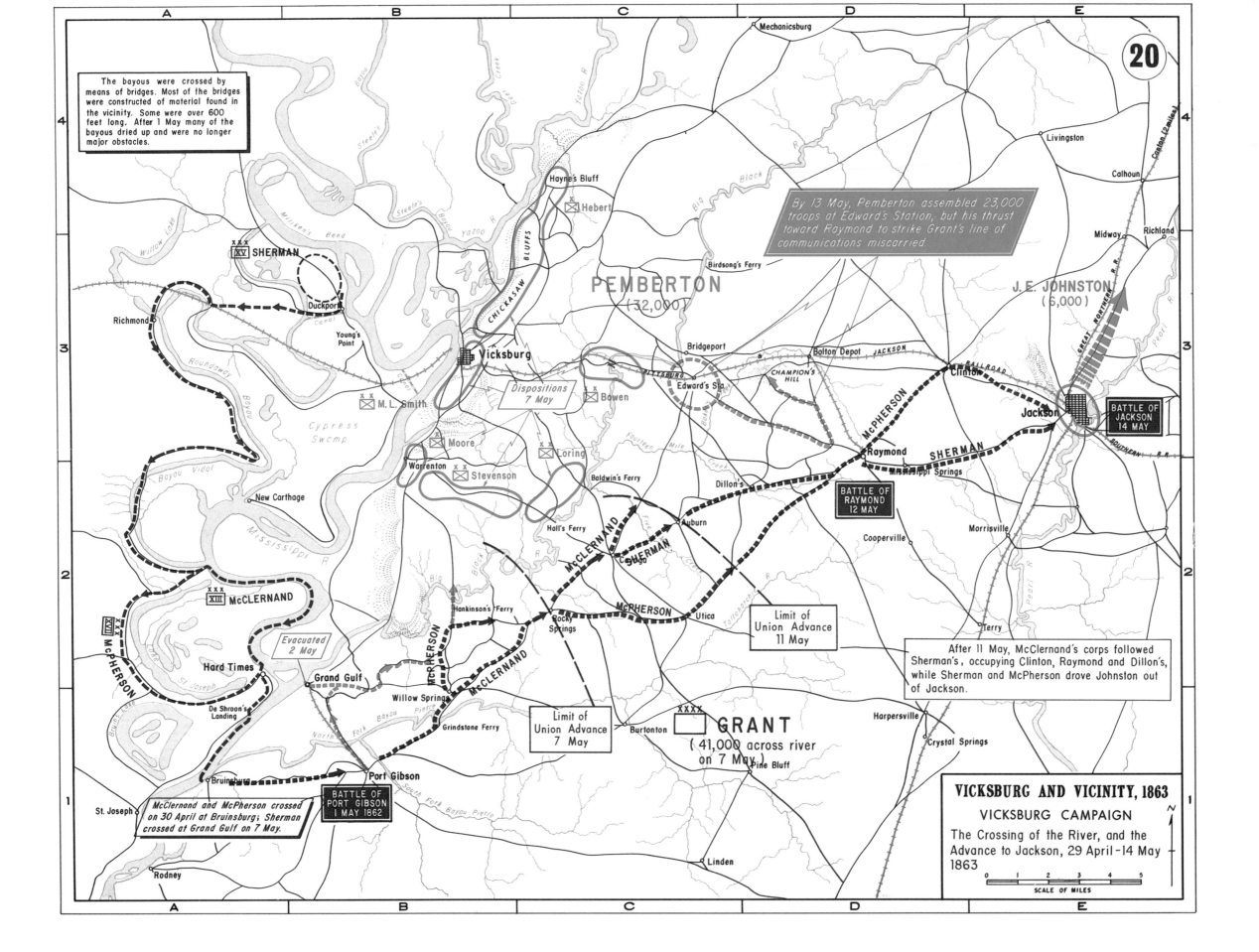

20

The bayous were crossed by means of bridges. Most of the bridges were constructed of material found in the vicinity. Some were over 600 feet long. After 1 May many of the bayous dried up and were no longer major obstacles.

By 13 May, Pemberton assembled 23,000 troops at Edward's Station, but his thrust toward Raymond to strike Grant's line of communications miscarried.

Mechanicsburg

Livingston

Calhoun

Midway   Richland

Haynes Bluff

Hebert

PEMBERTON
(32,000)

Birdsong's Ferry

J. E. JOHNSTON
(6,000)

CHICKASAW BLUFFS

Bridgeport   Bolton Depot   JACKSON

RAILROAD

Clinton

Vicksburg

Dispositions 7 May

Bowen

CHAMPION'S HILL

Edward's Sta.

McPHERSON

BATTLE OF JACKSON 14 MAY

Jackson

M. L. Smith

Moore

Loring

SHERMAN

Raymond

Mississippi Springs

SOUTHERN R.R.

BATTLE OF RAYMOND 12 MAY

Warrenton

Stevenson

Baldwin's Ferry

Dillon's

Morrisville

Hall's Ferry

Auburn

Cooperville

McCLERNAND   SHERMAN

McPHERSON

Utica

Limit of Union Advance 11 May

Terry

XXX
XV SHERMAN

Duckport

Young's Point

Richmond

Hankinson's Ferry

Rocky Springs

McPHERSON

After 11 May, McClernand's corps followed Sherman's, occupying Clinton, Raymond and Dillon's, while Sherman and McPherson drove Johnston out of Jackson.

XXX
XIII McCLERNAND

Evacuated 2 May

Hard Times

Grand Gulf

Willow Springs

McCLERNAND

XXXX
GRAND GULF

Harpersville

XXX
XVII
McPHERSON

De Shroon's Landing

Grindstone Ferry

Limit of Union Advance 7 May

Burtonton

Pine Bluff

GRANT
(41,000 across river on 7 May.)

Crystal Springs

St. Joseph

Bruinsburg

Port Gibson

McClernand and McPherson crossed on 30 April at Bruinsburg; Sherman crossed at Grand Gulf on 7 May.

BATTLE OF PORT GIBSON 1 MAY 1862

Rodney

Linden

VICKSBURG AND VICINITY, 1863

VICKSBURG CAMPAIGN

The Crossing of the River, and the Advance to Jackson, 29 April–14 May 1863

0 1 2 3 4 5
SCALE OF MILES

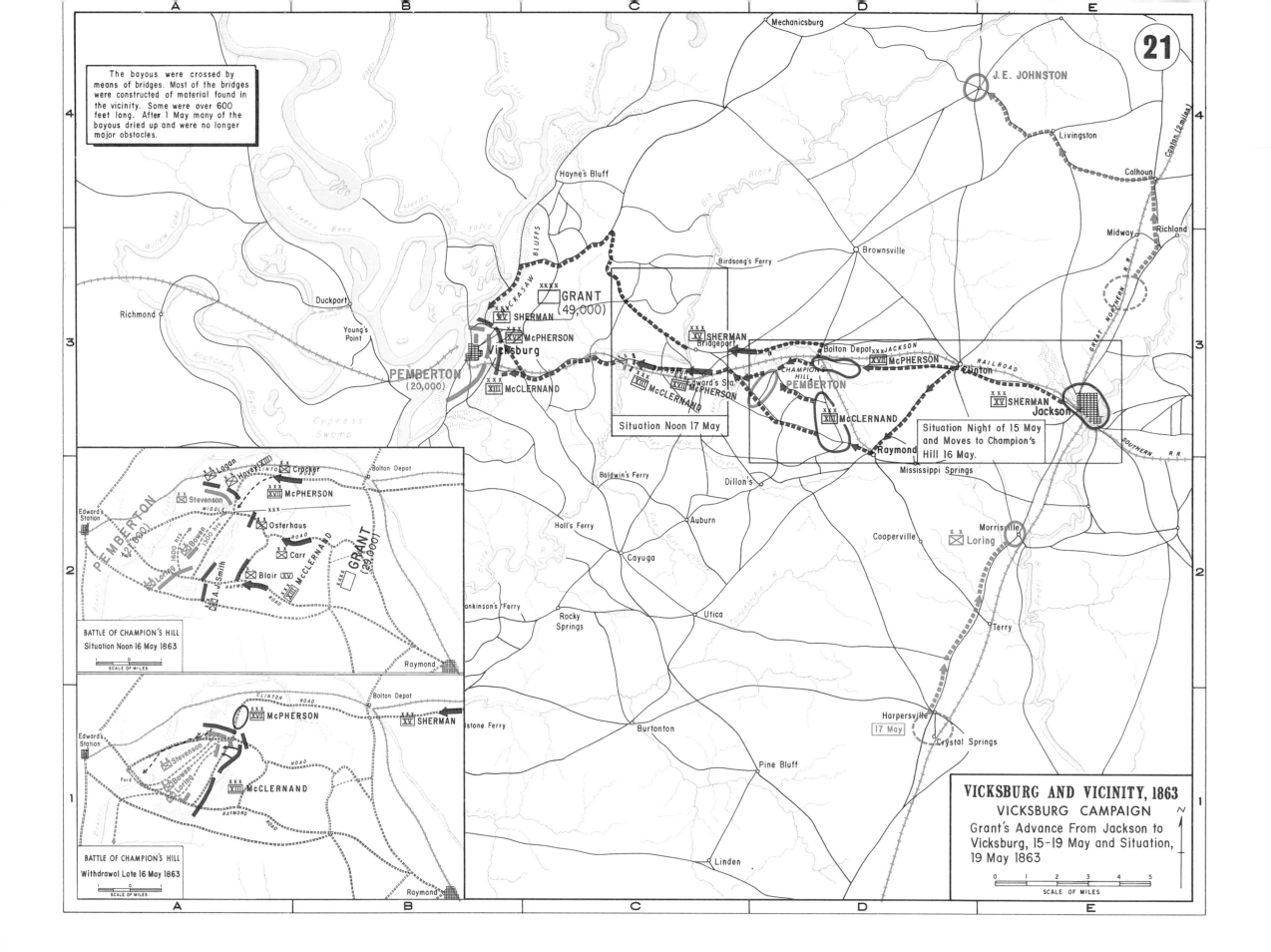

21

The bayous were crossed by means of bridges. Most of the bridges were constructed of material found in the vicinity. Some were over 600 feet long. After 1 May many of the bayous dried up and were no longer major obstacles.

J. E. JOHNSTON

Mechanicsburg

Livingston

Calhoun

Midway
Richland

Hayne's Bluff

Brownsville

Birdsong's Ferry

XXXX
GRANT
(49,000)

XXX
XV SHERMAN

XXX
XVII McPHERSON

Vicksburg

Bridgeport

XXX
XV SHERMAN

Bolton Depot

XXX JACKSON

XXX
XVII McPHERSON

Clinton

RAILROAD

PEMBERTON
(20,000)

PEMBERTON

CHAMPION'S HILL

XXX
XV SHERMAN
Jackson

XXX
XIII McCLERNAND

XVIII McCLERNAND

Edward's Sta.

XVII McPHERSON

XXX
XIII McCLERNAND

Situation Noon 17 May

Raymond

Situation Night of 15 May and Moves to Champion's Hill 16 May.

Mississippi Springs

Baldwin's Ferry

Dillon's

Morrisville

XX
Loring

Hall's Ferry

Auburn

Cooperville

Cayuga

Utica

Terry

Rocky Springs

Harpersville

17 May

Burtonton

Crystal Springs

Pine Bluff

Linden

BATTLE OF CHAMPION'S HILL
Situation Noon 16 May 1863

Logan
XX XIII
Hovey
Crocker

PEMBERTON

Stevenson

XXX
XVII McPHERSON

MIDDLE ROAD

XXX

Osterhaus

Bowen

GRANT
(29,000)

Loring

Carr

A. Smith

Blair (XV)

McCLERNAND

RAYMOND ROAD

Bolton Depot

Edward's Station

SCALE OF MILES

Raymond

BATTLE OF CHAMPION'S HILL
Withdrawal Late 16 May 1863

CLINTON ROAD

Bolton Depot

XXX
XVII McPHERSON

XV SHERMAN

Edward's Station

Stevenson

Bowen

Loring

Ford

XXX
XIII McCLERNAND

RAYMOND ROAD

Raymond

SCALE OF MILES

VICKSBURG AND VICINITY, 1863
VICKSBURG CAMPAIGN
Grant's Advance From Jackson to Vicksburg, 15-19 May and Situation, 19 May 1863

0 1 2 3 4 5
SCALE OF MILES

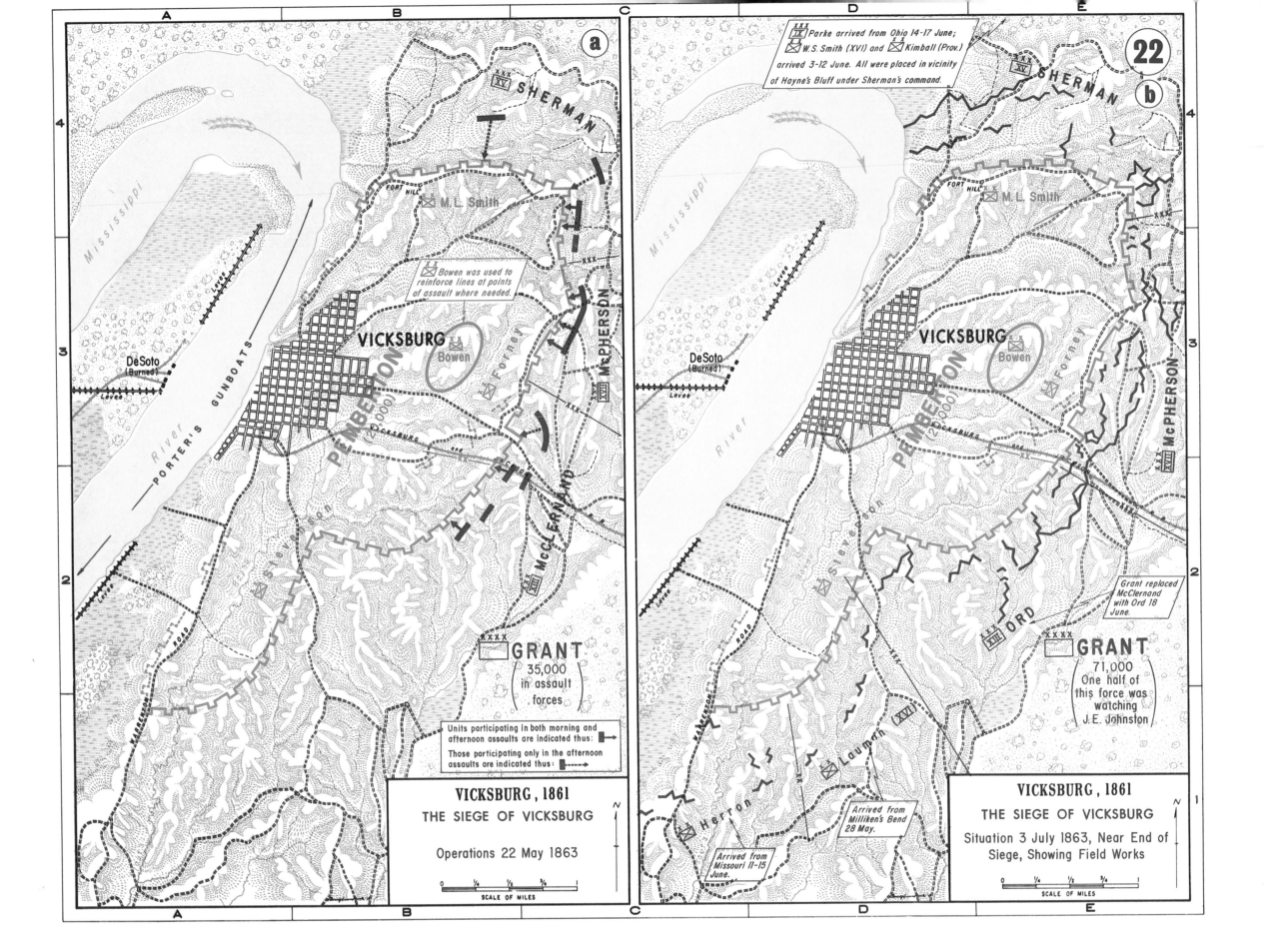

a

SHERMAN

FORT HILL

M.L. Smith

Bowen was used to
reinforce lines at points
of assault where needed.

VICKSBURG

Bowen

PEMBERTON
(20,000)

Forney

McPHERSON

DeSoto
(Burned)

Mississippi

River

PORTER'S GUNBOATS

Stevenson

McCLERNAND

XIII

JACKSON ROAD

GRANT
35,000
in assault
forces

Units participating in both morning and
afternoon assaults are indicated thus:

Those participating only in the afternoon
assaults are indicated thus:

VICKSBURG, 1861

THE SIEGE OF VICKSBURG

Operations 22 May 1863

SCALE OF MILES

22

b

Parke arrived from Ohio 14-17 June;
W.S. Smith (XVI) and Kimball (Prov.)
arrived 3-12 June. All were placed in vicinity
of Hayne's Bluff under Sherman's command.

XV

SHERMAN

FORT HILL

M.L. Smith

VICKSBURG

Bowen

PEMBERTON
(20,000)

Forney

McPHERSON

XVII

DeSoto
(Burned)

Mississippi

River

Levee

Stevenson

ORD

XIII

Grant replaced
McClernand
with Ord 18
June.

Lauman

XVI

Herron

Arrived from
Milliken's Bend
28 May.

Arrived from
Missouri 11-15
June.

GRANT
71,000
One half of
this force was
watching
J.E. Johnston

VICKSBURG, 1861

THE SIEGE OF VICKSBURG

Situation 3 July 1863, Near End of
Siege, Showing Field Works

SCALE OF MILES

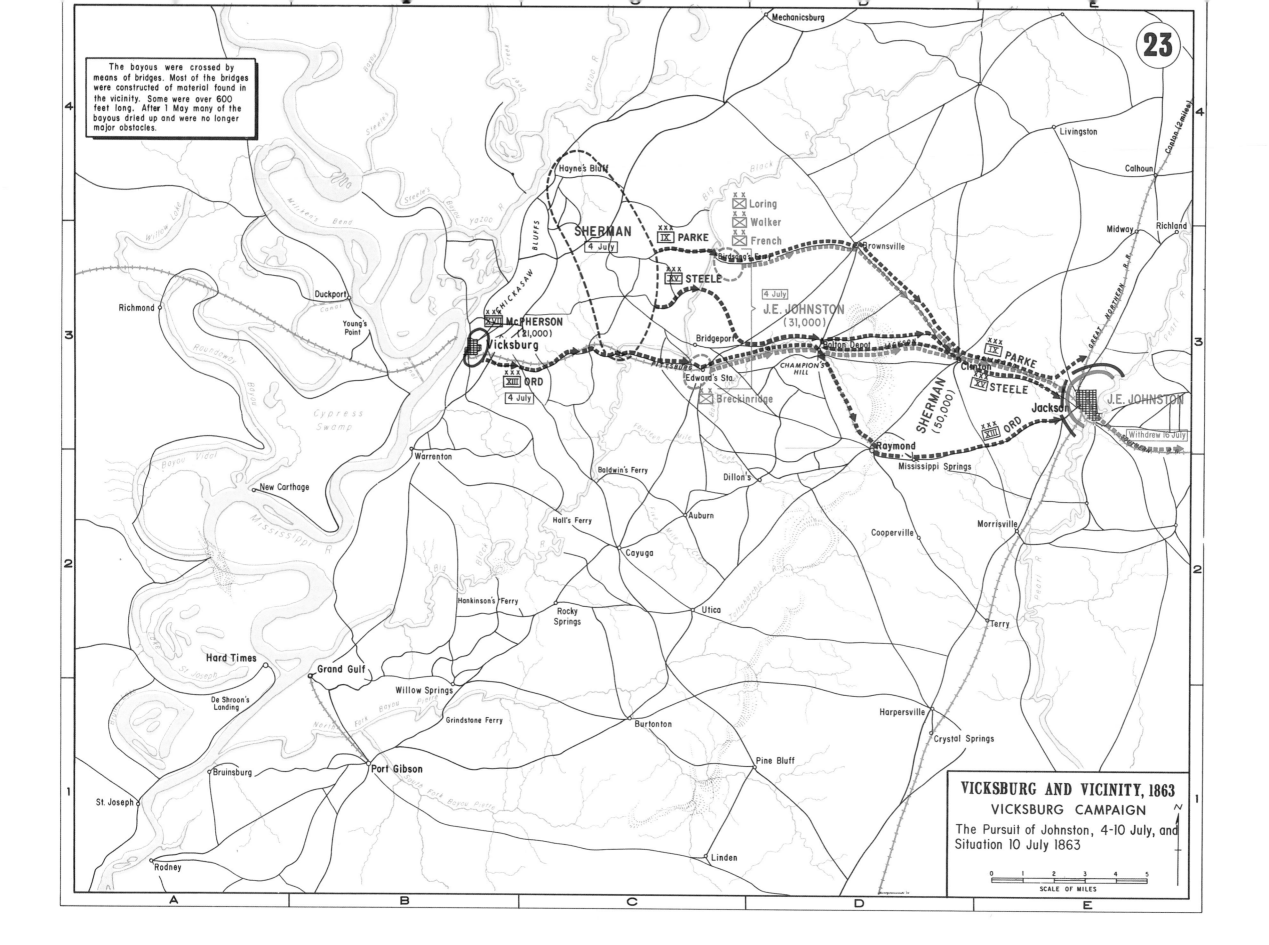

The bayous were crossed by means of bridges. Most of the bridges were constructed of material found in the vicinity. Some were over 600 feet long. After 1 May many of the bayous dried up and were no longer major obstacles.

SHERMAN
4 July

IX PARKE

XV STEELE

Loring
Walker
French

J.E. JOHNSTON
(31,000)

4 July

XVII McPHERSON
(31,000)

Vicksburg

XIII ORD
4 July

Bridgeport

Edward's Sta.

Breckinridge

CHAMPION'S HILL

Bolton Depot

IX PARKE
Clinton
XV STEELE

SHERMAN
(50,000)

J.E. JOHNSTON

Jackson

Withdrew 16 July

XIII ORD

Raymond

Mississippi Springs

VICKSBURG AND VICINITY, 1863
VICKSBURG CAMPAIGN
The Pursuit of Johnston, 4-10 July, and Situation 10 July 1863

0 1 2 3 4 5
SCALE OF MILES

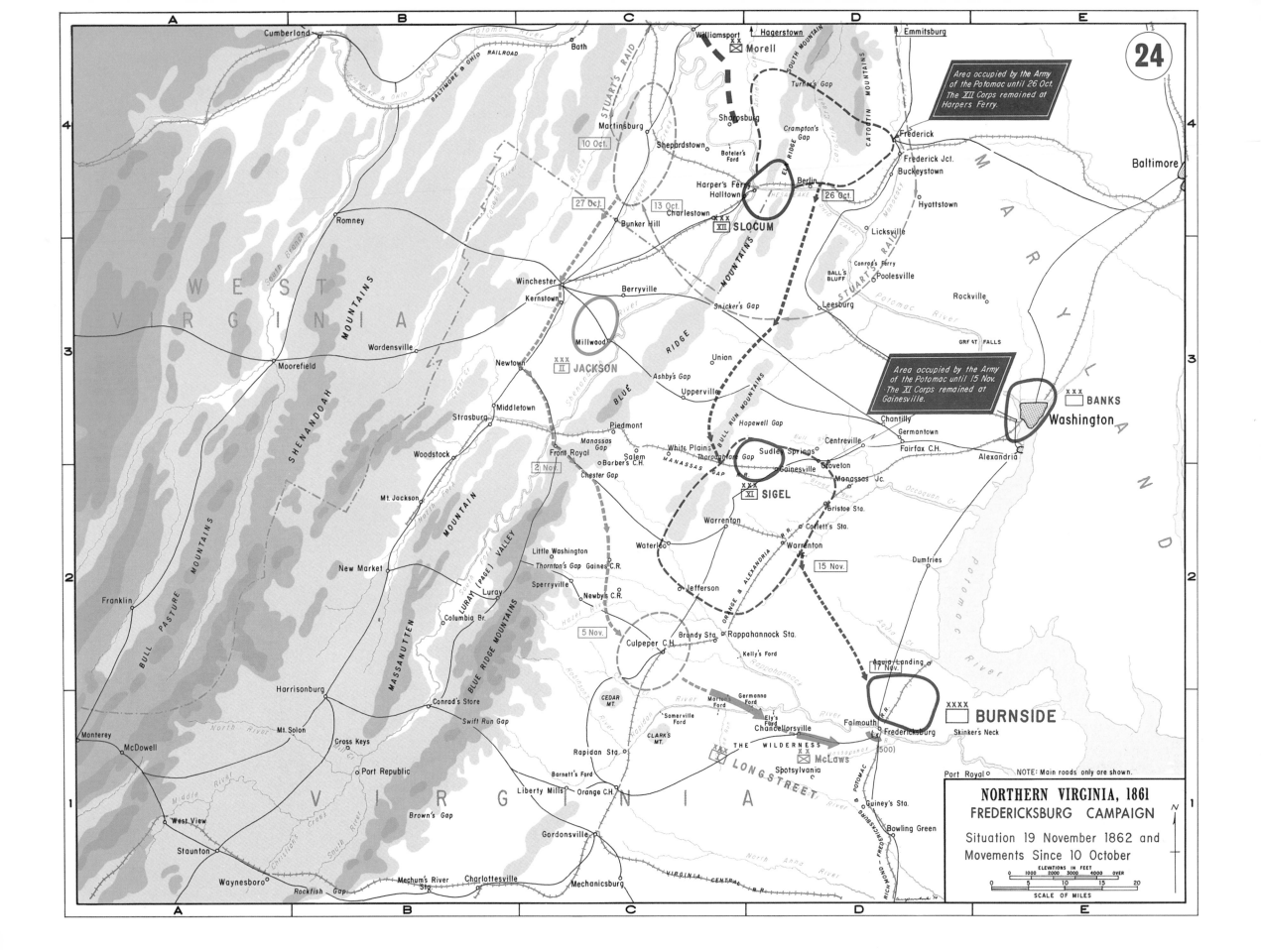

24

Area occupied by the Army of the Potomac until 26 Oct. The XII Corps remained at Harpers Ferry.

Area occupied by the Army of the Potomac until 15 Nov. The XI Corps remained at Gainesville.

NORTHERN VIRGINIA, 1861
FREDERICKSBURG CAMPAIGN

Situation 19 November 1862 and
Movements Since 10 October

NOTE: Main roads only are shown.

ELEVATIONS IN FEET
1000 2000 3000 4000 OVER

0 5 10 15 20
SCALE OF MILES

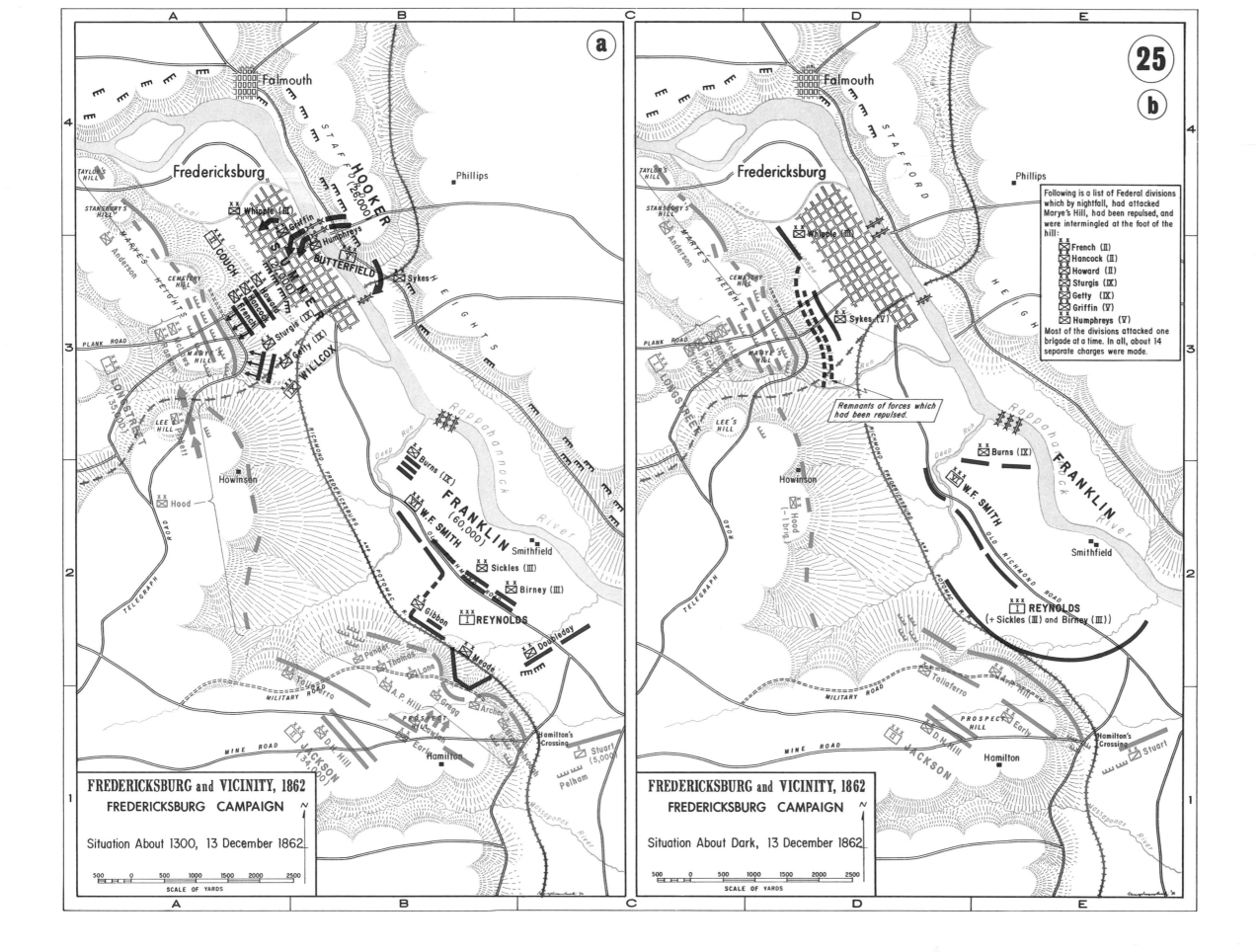

a

25

b

TAYLOR'S HILL

Falmouth

STAFFORD

Fredericksburg

Phillips

STANSBURY'S HILL

Canal

HOOKER (36,000)

XX Whipple (III)

Griffin

XX Humphreys

Anderson

X X COUCH

XX SUMNER (30,000)

BUTTERFIELD

Sykes

MARYE'S HEIGHTS

CEMETERY HILL

XX Hancock

XX Howell

XX French

Sturgis (IX)

HEIGHTS

PLANK ROAD

MARYE'S HILL

XX Getty (IX)

WILLCOX

LONGSTREET (35,000)

LEE HILL

Howinsen

XX Hood

Deep Run

Rappahannock River

XX Burns (IX)

FRANKLIN (60,000)

Smithfield

VI W.F. SMITH

XX Sickles (III)

XX Birney (III)

TELEGRAPH ROAD

RICHMOND FREDERICKSBURG RR

POTOMAC RR

XX Gibbon

XXX REYNOLDS

Pender

Thomas

Lane

XX Meade

XX Doubleday

A.P. Hill

Gregg

Archer

MILITARY ROAD

Telisro

PROSPECT HILL

Lawton

JACKSON (34,000)

D.H. Hill

Early

Hamilton

Hamilton's Crossing

Stuart (5,000)

MINE ROAD

Pelham

Massaponax River

FREDERICKSBURG and VICINITY, 1862
FREDERICKSBURG CAMPAIGN

Situation About 1300, 13 December 1862

500 0 500 1000 1500 2000 2500
SCALE OF YARDS

TAYLOR'S HILL

Falmouth

STAFFORD

Fredericksburg

Phillips

Following is a list of Federal divisions which by nightfall, had attacked Marye's Hill, had been repulsed, and were intermingled at the foot of the hill:

⊠ French (II)
⊠ Hancock (II)
⊠ Howard (II)
⊠ Sturgis (IX)
⊠ Getty (IX)
⊠ Griffin (V)
⊠ Humphreys (V)

Most of the divisions attacked one brigade at a time. In all, about 14 separate charges were made.

STANSBURY'S HILL

Canal

XX Whipple (III)

Anderson

MARYE'S HEIGHTS

CEMETERY HILL

Sykes (V)

PLANK ROAD

MARYE'S HILL

LONGSTREET

LEE'S HILL

Remnants of forces which had been repulsed.

HEIGHT

Deep Run

Rappahannock River

XX Burns (IX)

FRANKLIN

VI W.F. SMITH

Howinson

XX Hood (-1 brig.)

Smithfield

TELEGRAPH ROAD

RICHMOND FREDERICKSBURG RR

POTOMAC RR

I REYNOLDS

(+ Sickles (III) and Birney (III))

MILITARY ROAD

Taliaferro

A.P. Hill

PROSPECT HILL

JACKSON

D.H. Hill

Early

Hamilton

Hamilton's Crossing

Stuart

MINE ROAD

Massaponax River

FREDERICKSBURG and VICINITY, 1862
FREDERICKSBURG CAMPAIGN

Situation About Dark, 13 December 1862

500 0 500 1000 1500 2000 2500
SCALE OF YARDS

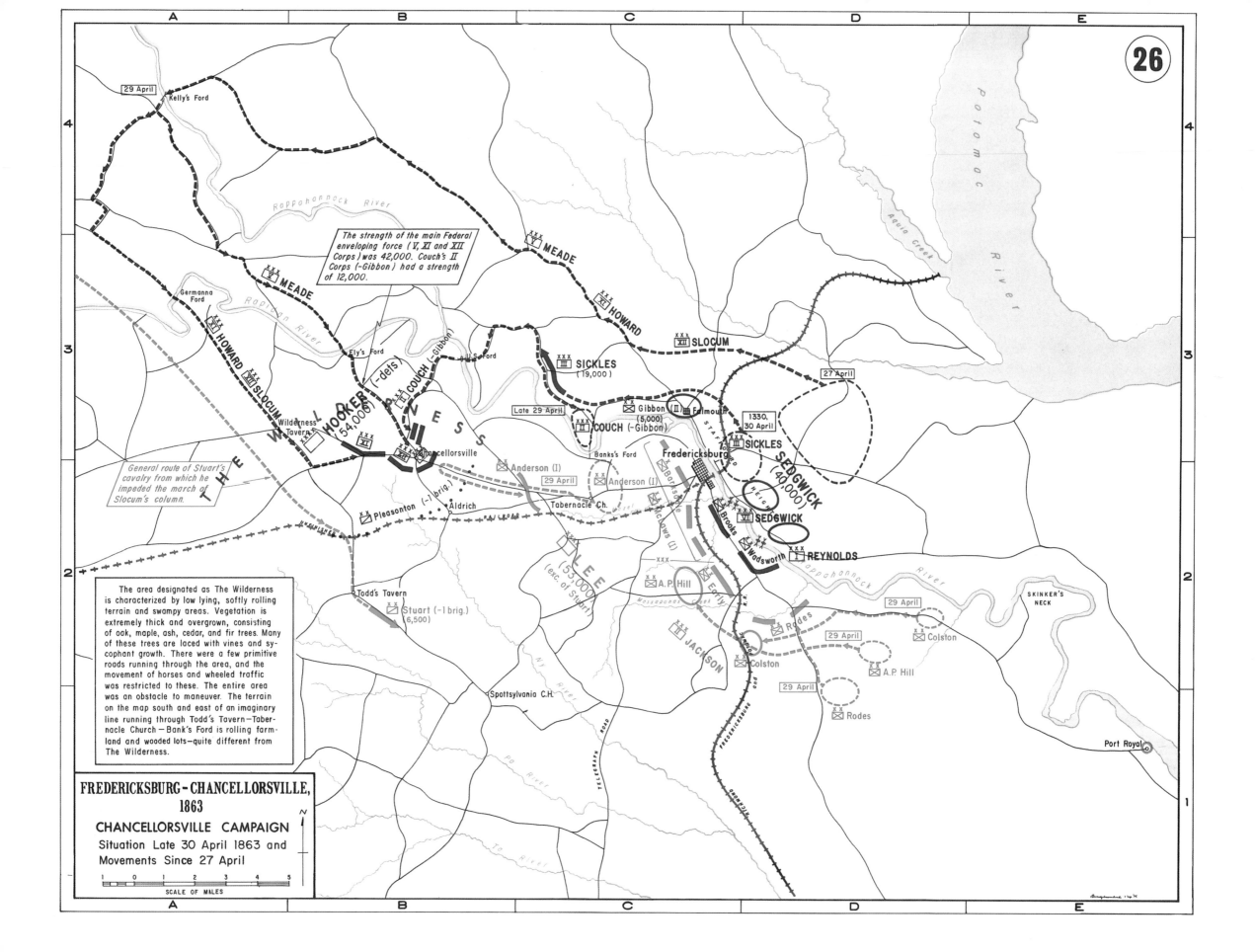

26

The strength of the main Federal enveloping force (V, XI and XII Corps) was 42,000. Couch's II Corps (-Gibbon) had a strength of 12,000.

General route of Stuart's cavalry from which he impeded the march of Slocum's column.

The area designated as The Wilderness is characterized by low lying, softly rolling terrain and swampy areas. Vegetation is extremely thick and overgrown, consisting of oak, maple, ash, cedar, and fir trees. Many of these trees are laced with vines and sycophant growth. There were a few primitive roads running through the area, and the movement of horses and wheeled traffic was restricted to these. The entire area was an obstacle to maneuver. The terrain on the map south and east of an imaginary line running through Todd's Tavern — Tabernacle Church — Bank's Ford is rolling farmland and wooded lots — quite different from The Wilderness.

29 April — Kelly's Ford
Rappahannock River
MEADE
Germanna Ford
Rapidan River
HOWARD
SLOCUM
Ely's Ford
Wilderness Tavern
HOOKER 54,000
COUCH (-defs.)
Chancellorsville
Pleasonton (-1 brig.)
Aldrich
Todd's Tavern
Stuart (-1 brig.) 6,500
Spottsylvania C.H.

MEADE
HOWARD
SLOCUM
U.S. Ford
SICKLES (19,000)
Late 29 April
Gibbon (5,000)
COUCH (-Gibbon)
Banks's Ford
Anderson (I)
29 April
Anderson (I)
Tabernacle Ch.
LEE (53,000) (exc. of Stuart)
A.P. Hill
JACKSON
Colston
Rodes

Potomac River
Aquia Creek
27 April
1330, 30 April
Fredericksburg
SICKLES
SEDGWICK (40,000)
McGowan's
SEDGWICK
Wadsworth
REYNOLDS
Early
Rodes
29 April
Colston
29 April
A.P. Hill
29 April
Rodes
SKINKER'S NECK
Port Royal

FREDERICKSBURG — CHANCELLORSVILLE, 1863

CHANCELLORSVILLE CAMPAIGN

Situation Late 30 April 1863 and Movements Since 27 April

1 0 1 2 3 4 5
SCALE OF MILES

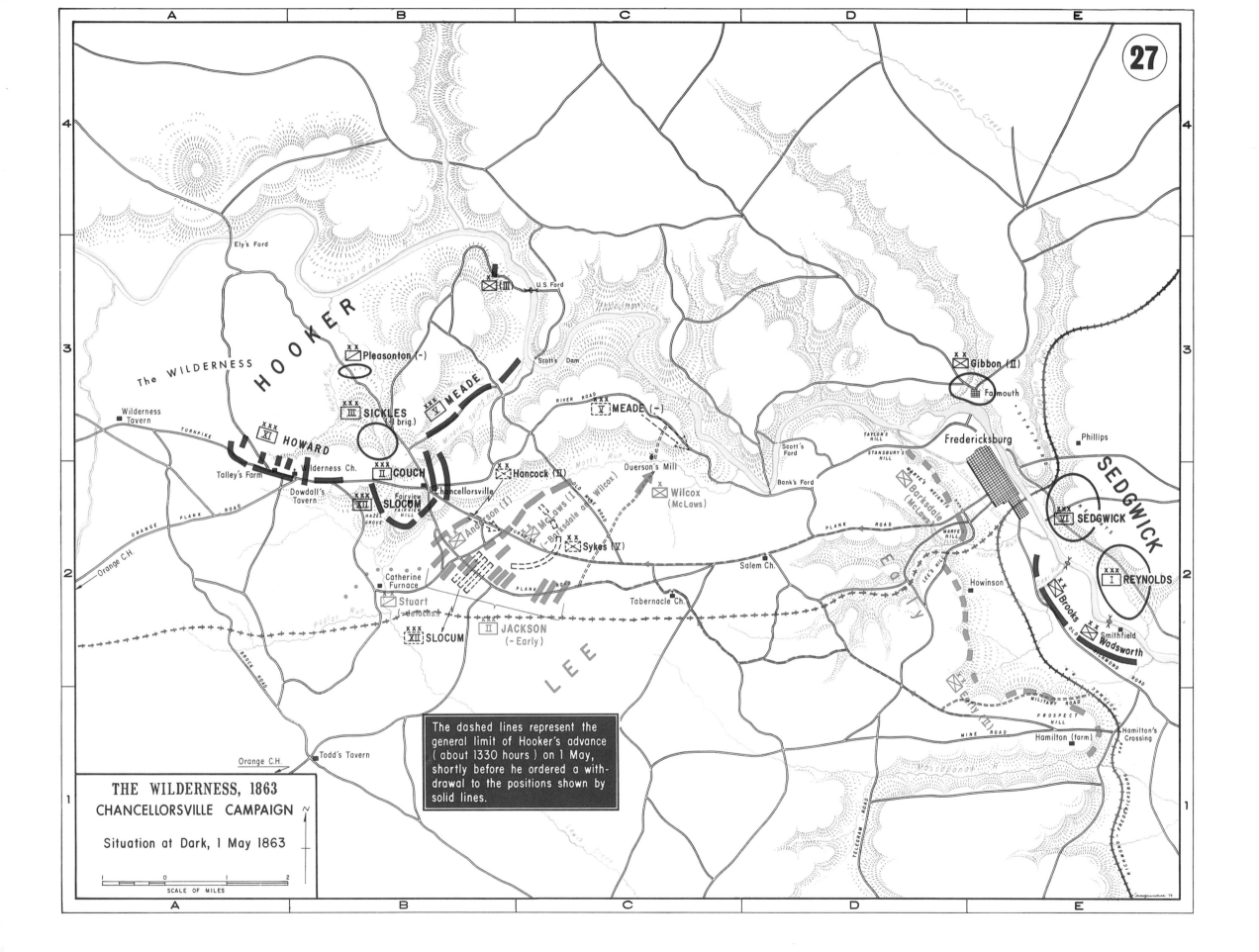

27

THE WILDERNESS, 1863
CHANCELLORSVILLE CAMPAIGN

Situation at Dark, 1 May 1863

The dashed lines represent the general limit of Hooker's advance (about 1330 hours) on 1 May, shortly before he ordered a withdrawal to the positions shown by solid lines.

SCALE OF MILES

The WILDERNESS

HOOKER

LEE

SEDGWICK

Ely's Ford

U.S. Ford

Scott's Dam

Scott's Ford

Bank's Ford

Falmouth

Fredericksburg

Phillips

Pleasonton (-)

MEADE

Gibbon (II)

MEADE (-)

SICKLES (1 brig.)

HOWARD

Wilderness Tavern

TURNPIKE

Talley's Farm

Wilderness Ch.

Dowdall's Tavern

COUCH

Fairview Hill

SLOCUM

Hazel Grove

Chancellorsville

Hancock (II)

Duerson's Mill

Wilcox (McLaws)

Taylor's Hill

Stansbury's Hill

Marye's Heights

Barksdale (McLaws)

SEDGWICK

REYNOLDS

Orange C.H.

ORANGE PLANK ROAD

Catherine Furnace

Stuart (detachs.)

Anderson (I)

McLaws (- Barksdale or Wilcox)

Sykes (V)

Salem Ch.

PLANK ROAD

Tabernacle Ch.

Marye Hill

Howinson

Brooks

Smithfield

Wadsworth

SLOCUM

JACKSON (- Early)

BROCK ROAD

Orange C.H.

Todd's Tavern

TELEGRAPH ROAD

Early (II)

Prospect Hill

MINE ROAD

MILITARY ROAD

Hamilton (farm)

Hamilton's Crossing

RICHMOND-FREDERICKSBURG

River Road

Wilderness Tavern

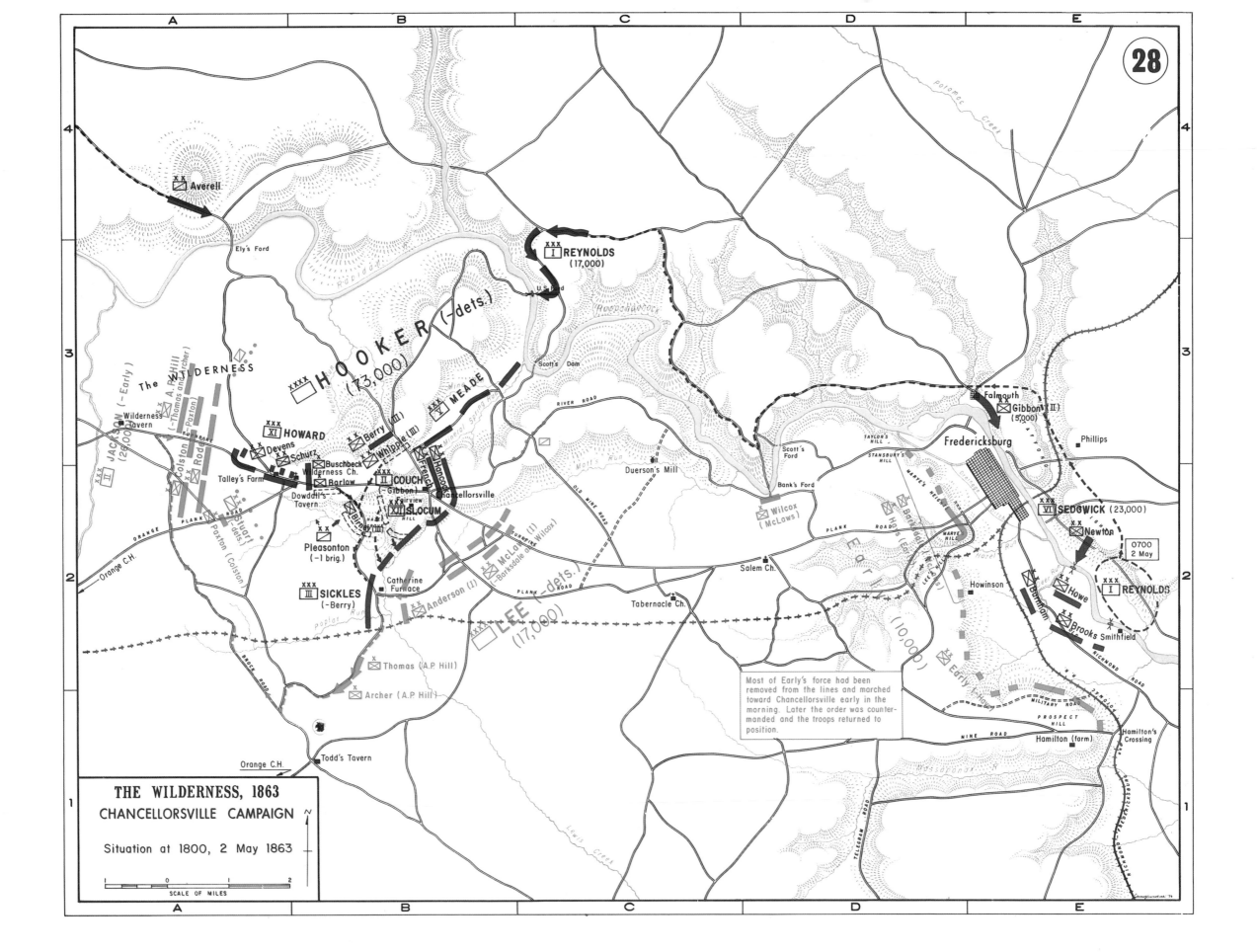

THE WILDERNESS, 1863
CHANCELLORSVILLE CAMPAIGN

Situation at 1800, 2 May 1863

SCALE OF MILES

Most of Early's force had been removed from the lines and marched toward Chancellorsville early in the morning. Later the order was countermanded and the troops returned to position.

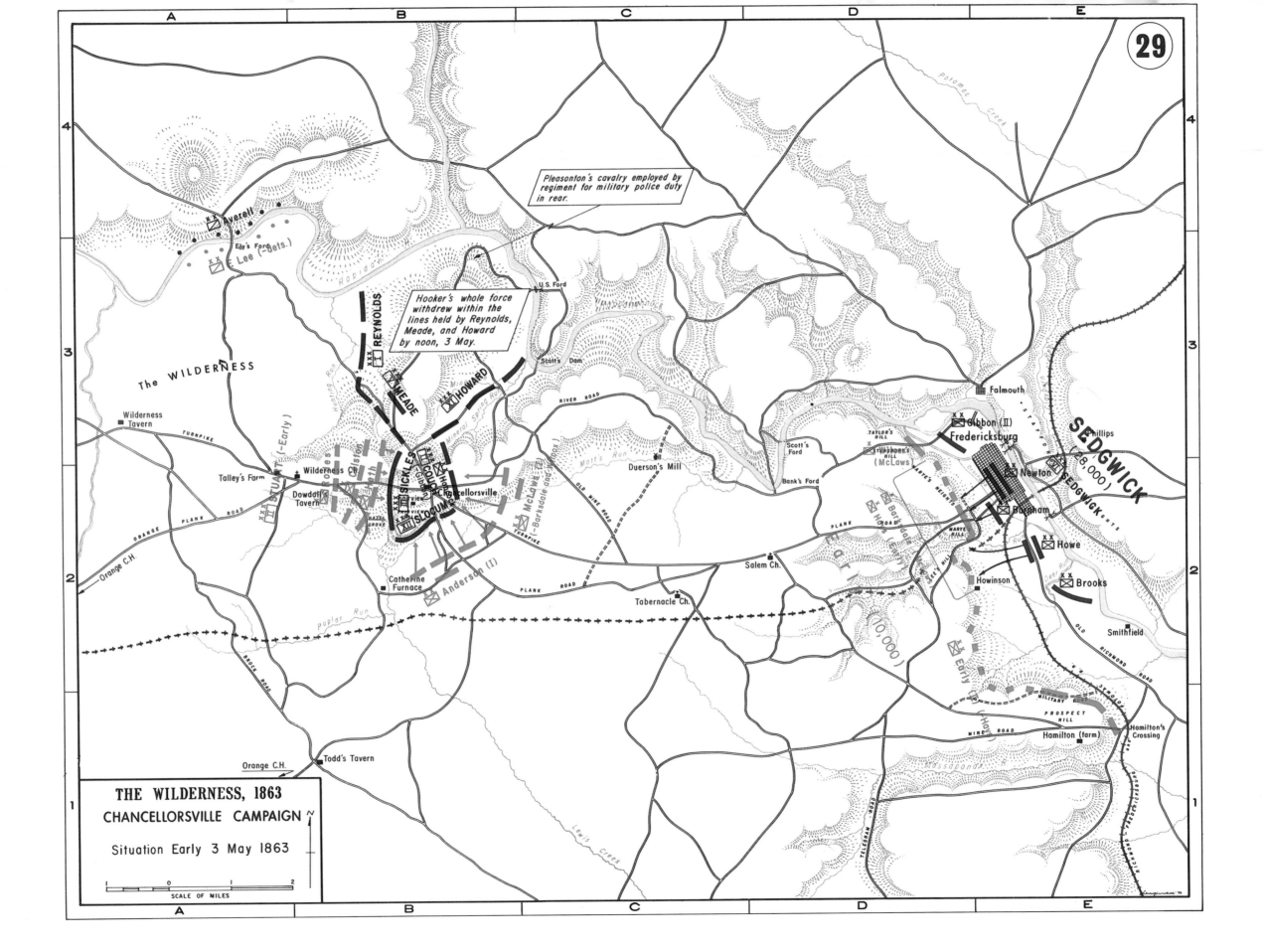

29

Pleasonton's cavalry employed by regiment for military police duty in rear.

Hooker's whole force withdrew within the lines held by Reynolds, Meade, and Howard by noon, 3 May.

The WILDERNESS

Wilderness Tavern

TURNPIKE

Talley's Farm

Dowdall's Tavern

Catherine Furnace

Orange C.H.

ORANGE PLANK ROAD

BROCK ROAD

Orange C.H.

Todd's Tavern

Averell

Ely's Ford

F. Lee (-dets.)

REYNOLDS

MEADE

HOWARD

SICKLES

COUCH

SLOCUM

Chancellorsville

Anderson (I)

STUART (-Early)

Hazel Grove

McLaws (-Barksdale and Wilcox)

U.S. Ford

Scott's Dam

RIVER ROAD

Mott's Run

Duerson's Mill

Scott's Ford

Bank's Ford

OLD MINE ROAD

Salem Ch.

PLANK ROAD

Tabernacle Ch.

Falmouth

Gibbon (II)

Fredericksburg

TAYLOR'S HILL

Wilcox's Hill (McLaws)

Newton

Burnham

Howe

Brooks

Howinson

SEDGWICK
(28,000)

Phillips

SEDGWICK HEIGHTS

Barksdale (Early)

HOWE HILL

MARYE'S HEIGHTS

HAZEL HILL

Early (-) (10,000)

Early (-) (Hays)

Smithfield

Hamilton (farm)

Hamilton's Crossing

PROSPECT HILL

MILITARY ROAD

MINE ROAD

TELEGRAPH ROAD

OLD RICHMOND ROAD

Massaponax R.

Lewis Creek

Potomac Creek

Poplar Run

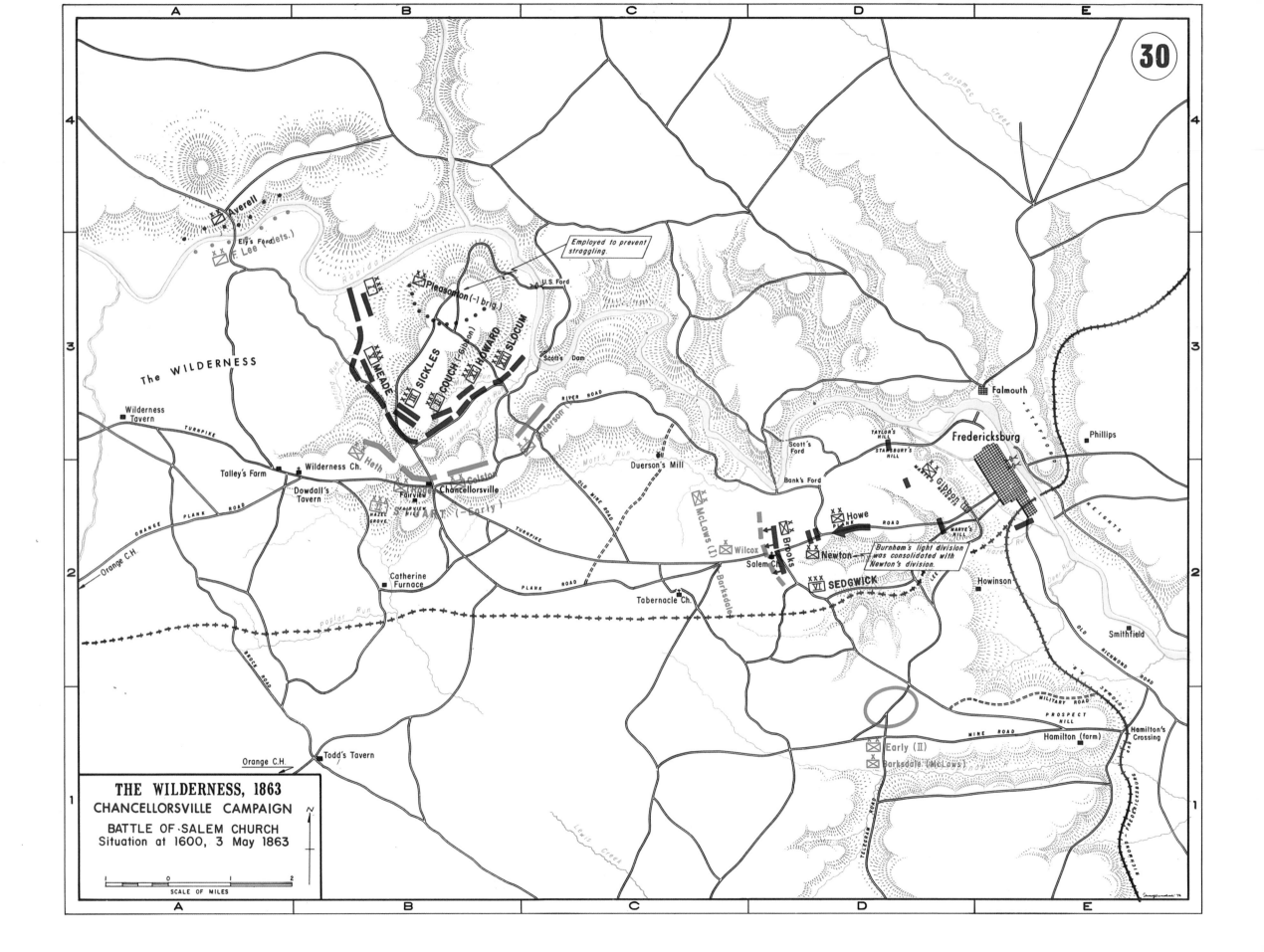

THE WILDERNESS, 1863
CHANCELLORSVILLE CAMPAIGN
BATTLE OF·SALEM CHURCH
Situation at 1600, 3 May 1863

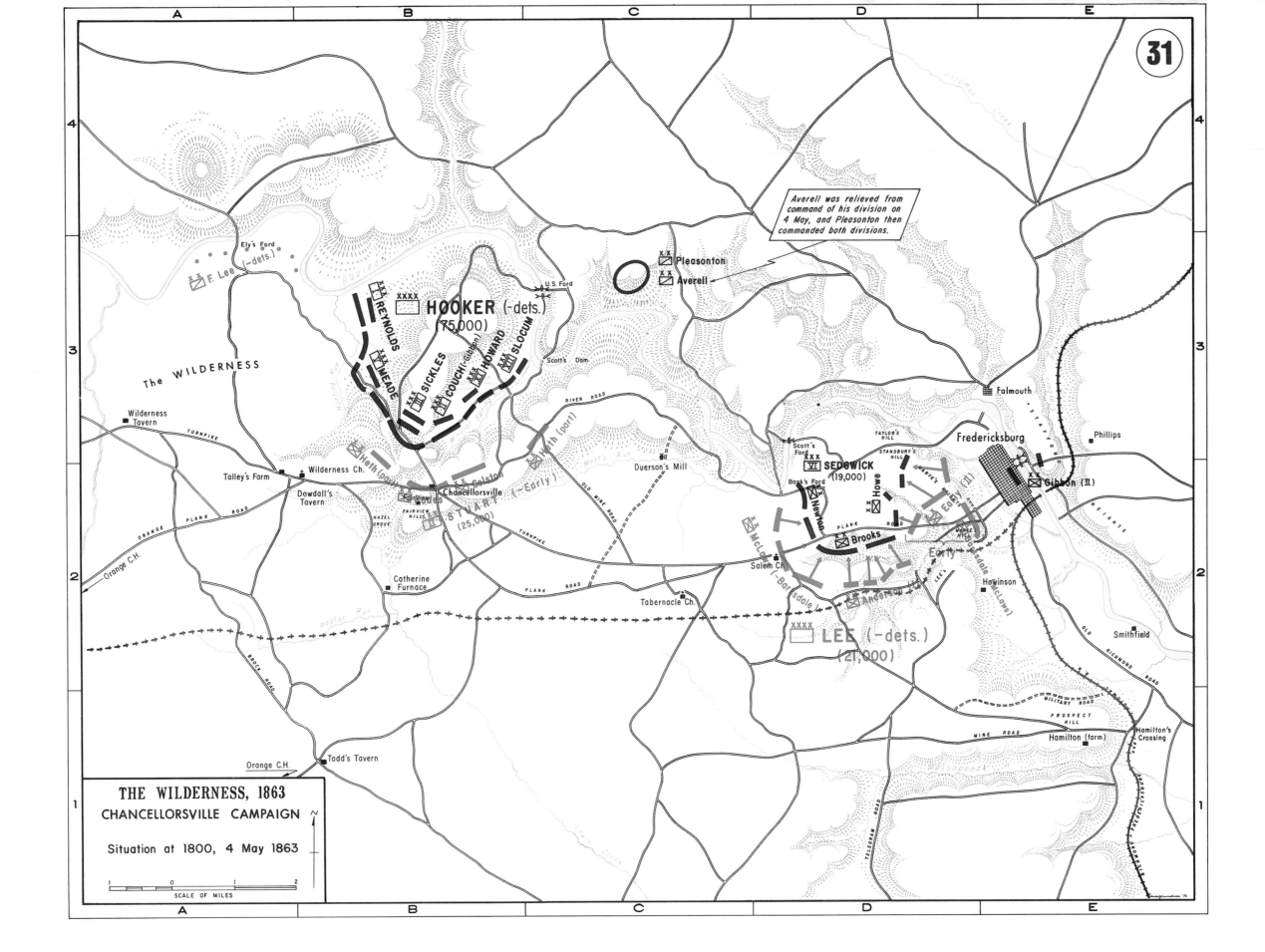

31

Averell was relieved from command of his division on 4 May, and Pleasonton then commanded both divisions.

Ely's Ford

F. Lee (-dets.)

Rapidan

U.S. Ford

XX Pleasonton

XX Averell

XXX REYNOLDS

XXXX HOOKER (-dets.) (75,000)

Scott's Dam

The WILDERNESS

XXX MEADE

XX SICKLES

XX COUCH (-Gibbon)

XXX HOWARD

XXX SLOCUM

River Road

Falmouth

Wilderness Tavern

TURNPIKE

Heth (part)

Heth (part)

Mott's Run

Duerson's Mill

Scott's Ford

Taylor's Hill

Stansbury's Hill

Fredericksburg

Phillips

Talley's Farm

Wilderness Ch.

Colston

Chancellorsville

Stuart (-Early)

XXX SEDGWICK (19,000)

Bank's Ford

XX Newton

XX Howe

XX Gibbon (II)

Dowdall's Tavern

Fairview

HAZEL GROVE

FAIRVIEW HILLS

STUART (25,000)

Old Mine Road

Marye's Heights

Early (II)

XX Brooks

PLANK ROAD

Early

ORANGE PLANK ROAD

Catherine Furnace

TURNPIKE

Salem Ch.

McLaws

Salem Ch. (-Barksdale)

Anderson

Lee's

Howinson

Orange C.H.

PLANK ROAD

Tabernacle Ch.

Poplar Run

XXXX LEE (-dets.) (21,000)

Smithfield

BROCK ROAD

Orange C.H.

Todd's Tavern

OLD RICHMOND ROAD

Prospect Hill

Hamilton (farm)

MINE ROAD

MILITARY ROAD

Hamilton's Crossing

TELEGRAPH ROAD

THE WILDERNESS, 1863
CHANCELLORSVILLE CAMPAIGN

Situation at 1800, 4 May 1863

SCALE OF MILES
1   0   1   2

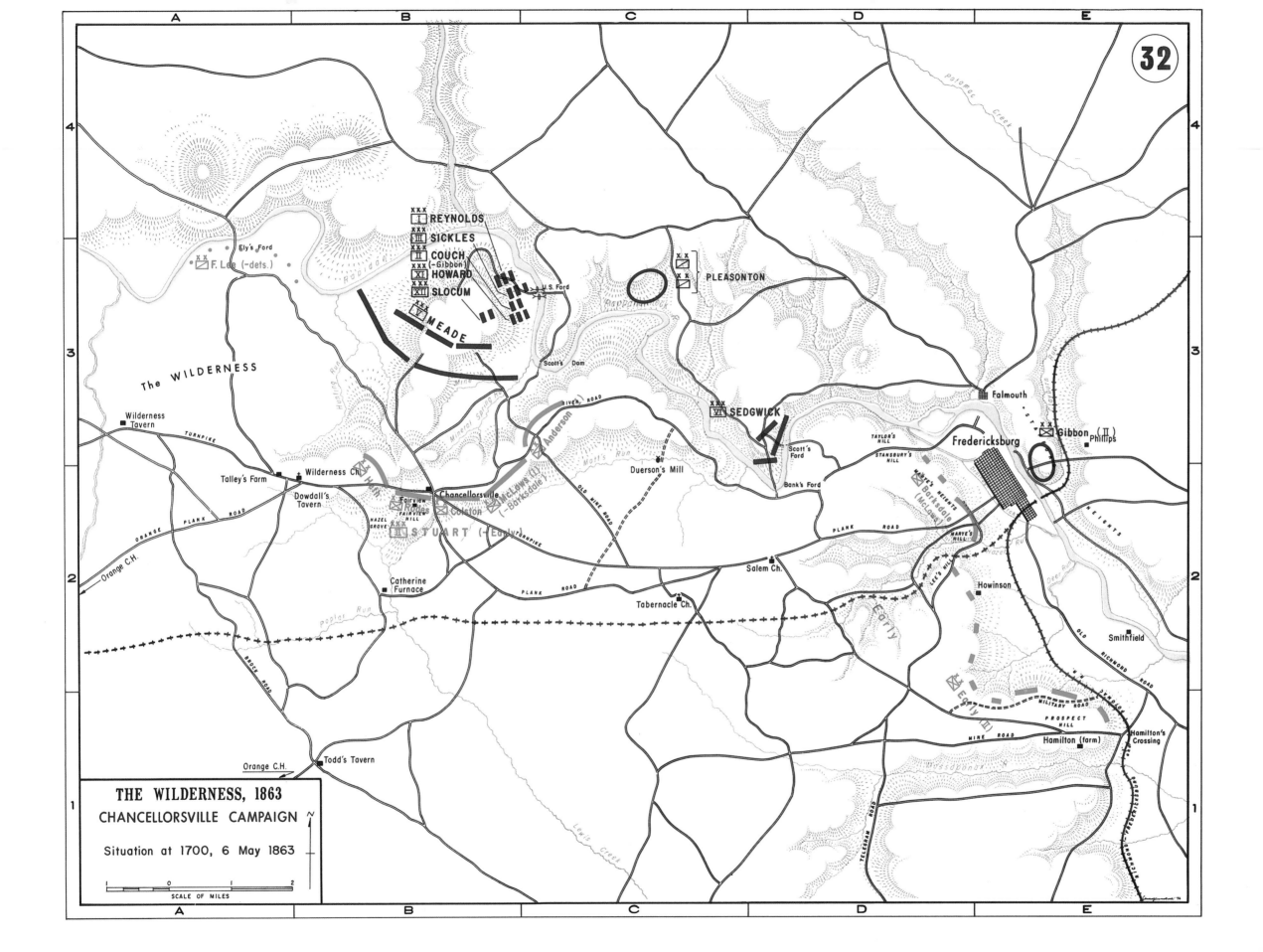

32

XXX I REYNOLDS
XXX III SICKLES
XXX II COUCH
XXX (- Gibbon)
XXX XI HOWARD
XXX XII SLOCUM
XXX V MEADE

F. Lee (-dets.)

Ely's Ford

U.S. Ford

PLEASONTON

Rappahannock

Scott's Dam

The WILDERNESS

RIVER ROAD

Falmouth

Wilderness Tavern

TURNPIKE

XXX VI SEDGWICK

TAYLOR'S HILL

Wilderness Ch.

Anderson

Scott's Ford

STANSBURY'S HILL

Fredericksburg

Gibbon (II)

Phillips

Talley's Farm

Dowdall's Tavern

Fairview

Chancellorsville

McLaws (I) (-Barksdale)

Duerson's Mill

Bank's Ford

Marye's Heights

Barksdale (McLaws)

ORANGE PLANK ROAD

Hill

Rodes

Colston

OLD NINE ROAD

HEIGHTS

Orange C.H.

HAZEL GROVE

FAIRVIEW HILL

STUART (- Early)

TURNPIKE

PLANK ROAD

Salem Ch.

MARYE'S HILL

Lee's Hill

Howison

Catherine Furnace

PLANK ROAD

Tabernacle Ch.

Early

Smithfield

Poplar Run

OLD RICHMOND ROAD

PROSPECT HILL

MILITARY ROAD

Early (II)

NINE ROAD

Todd's Tavern

Orange C.H.

BROCK ROAD

Lewis Creek

TELEGRAPH ROAD

Hamilton (farm)

Hamilton's Crossing

THE WILDERNESS, 1863
CHANCELLORSVILLE CAMPAIGN

Situation at 1700, 6 May 1863

SCALE OF MILES
1 0 1 2

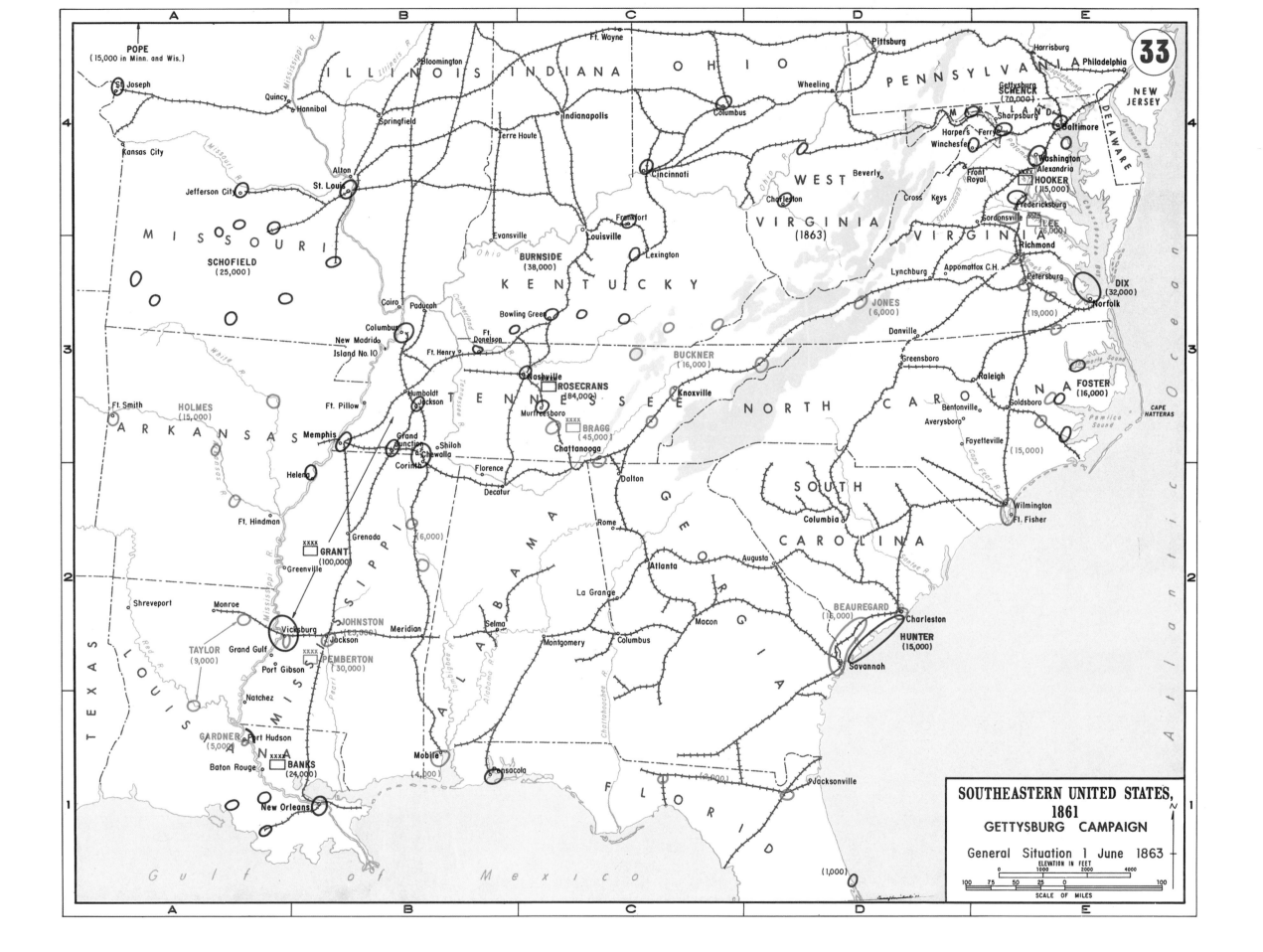

SOUTHEASTERN UNITED STATES, 1861
GETTYSBURG CAMPAIGN
General Situation 1 June 1863

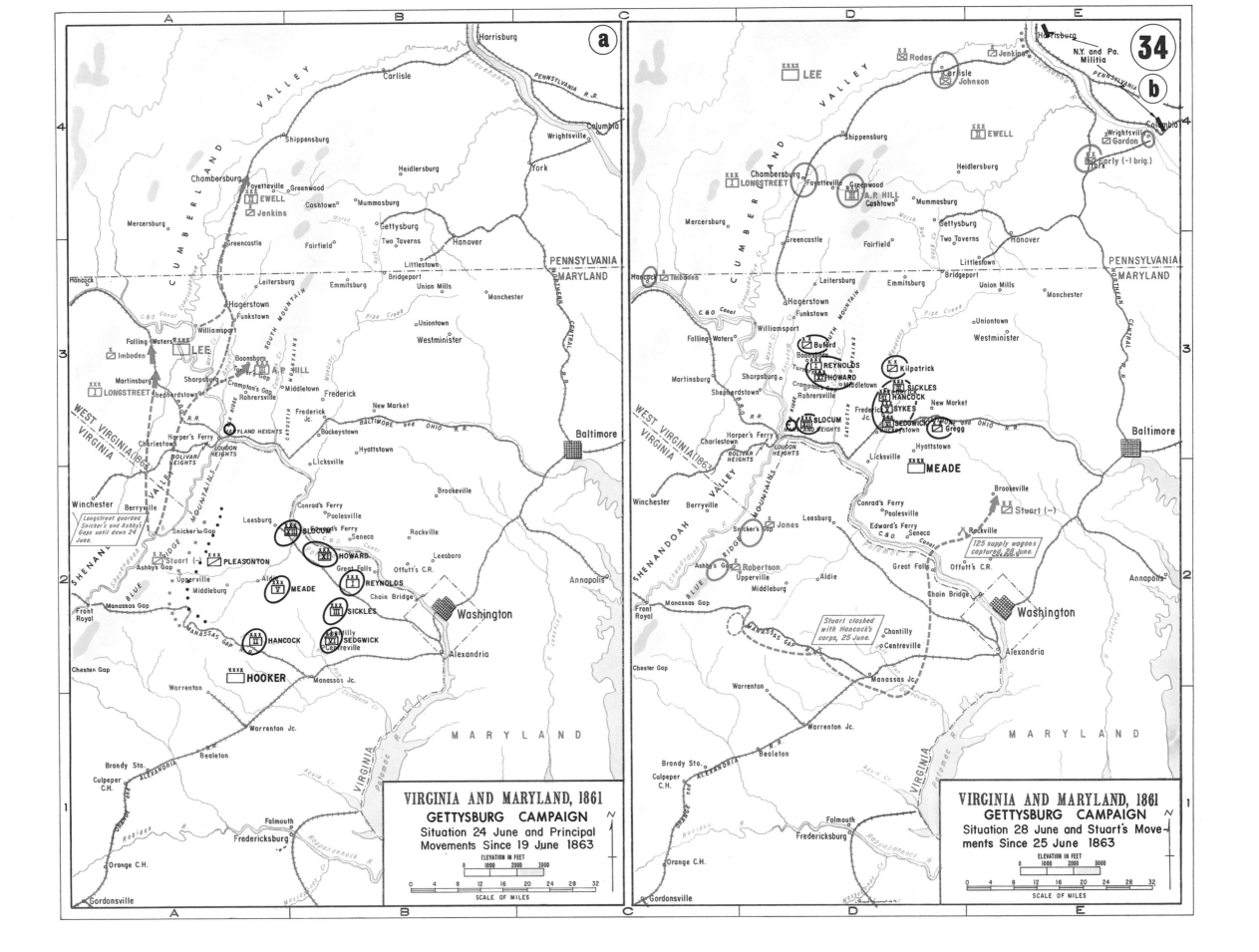

VIRGINIA AND MARYLAND, 1861

GETTYSBURG CAMPAIGN

Situation 24 June and Principal
Movements Since 19 June 1863

VIRGINIA AND MARYLAND, 1861

GETTYSBURG CAMPAIGN

Situation 28 June and Stuart's Movements Since 25 June 1863

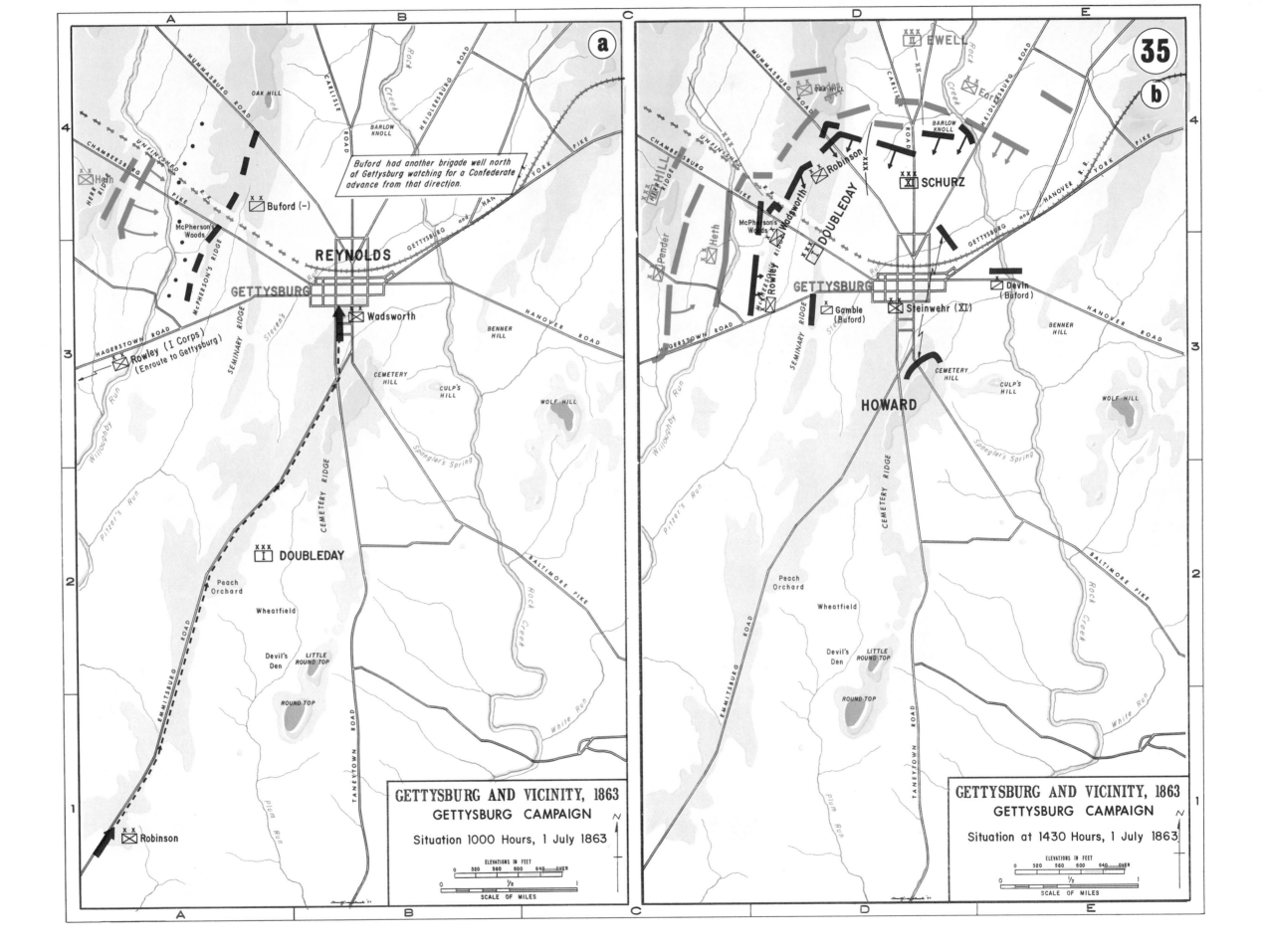

a

OAK HILL

BARLOW
KNOLL

Buford had another brigade well north
of Gettysburg watching for a Confederate
advance from that direction.

Heth

Buford (−)

McPherson's
Woods

REYNOLDS

GETTYSBURG

Wadsworth

Rowley (I Corps)
(Enroute to Gettysburg)

BENNER
HILL

WOLF HILL

CEMETERY
HILL

CULP'S
HILL

DOUBLEDAY

Peach
Orchard

Wheatfield

Devil's
Den

LITTLE
ROUND TOP

ROUND TOP

Robinson

GETTYSBURG AND VICINITY, 1863
GETTYSBURG CAMPAIGN

Situation 1000 Hours, 1 July 1863

ELEVATIONS IN FEET
520 560 600 640 OVER

0   ½   1
SCALE OF MILES

b

35

EWELL

Earl

BARLOW
KNOLL

Robinson

SCHURZ

HETH HILL

Pender

Heth

McPherson's
Woods

Wadsworth

DOUBLEDAY

Rowley

McPherson

GETTYSBURG

Gamble
(Buford)

Steinwehr (XI)

Devin
(Buford)

BENNER
HILL

WOLF HILL

CEMETERY
HILL

CULP'S
HILL

HOWARD

Peach
Orchard

Wheatfield

Devil's
Den

LITTLE
ROUND TOP

ROUND TOP

GETTYSBURG AND VICINITY, 1863
GETTYSBURG CAMPAIGN

Situation at 1430 Hours, 1 July 1863

ELEVATIONS IN FEET
520 560 600 640 OVER

0   ½   1
SCALE OF MILES

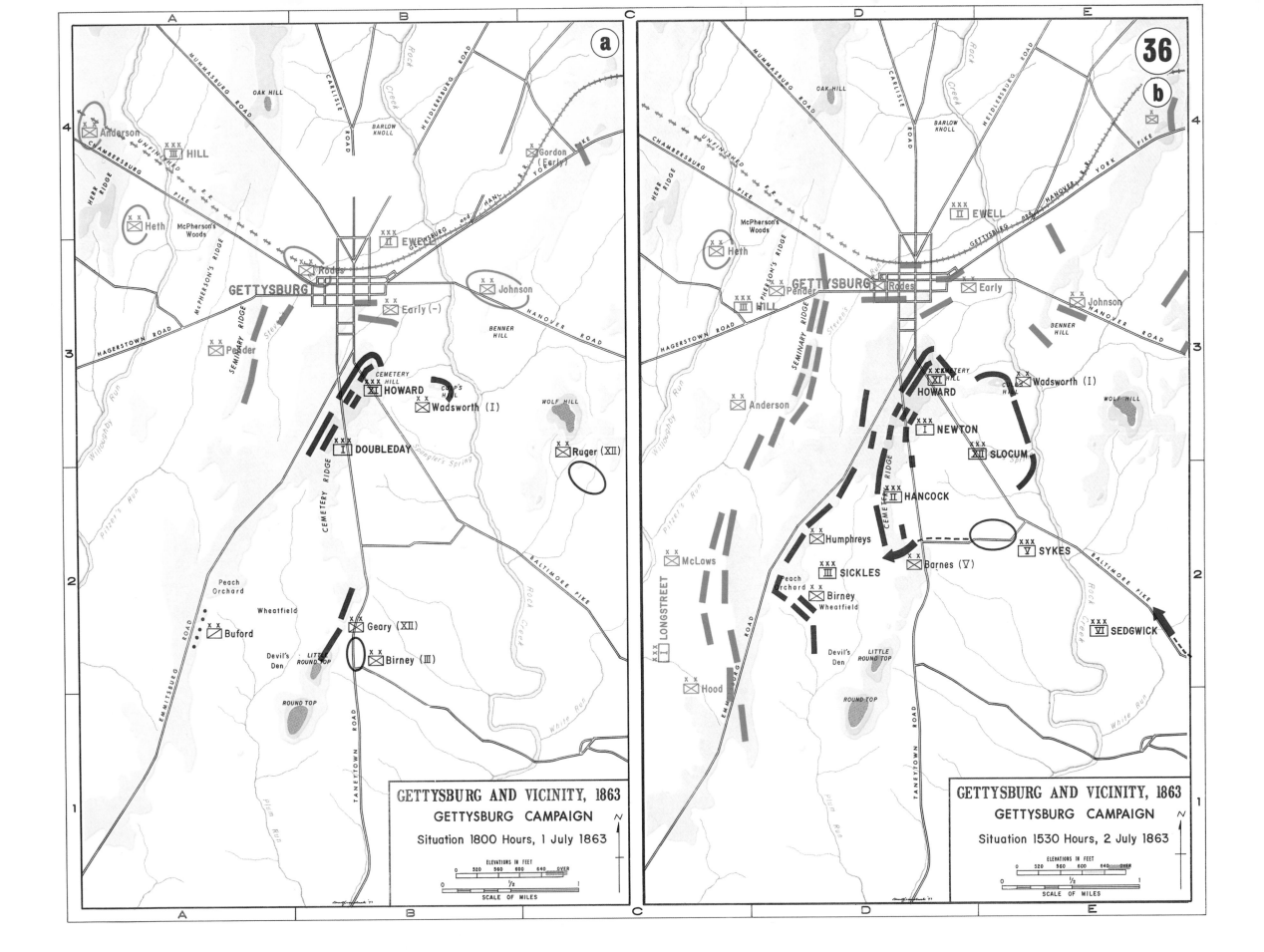

GETTYSBURG AND VICINITY, 1863
GETTYSBURG CAMPAIGN
Situation 1800 Hours, 1 July 1863

GETTYSBURG AND VICINITY, 1863
GETTYSBURG CAMPAIGN
Situation 1530 Hours, 2 July 1863

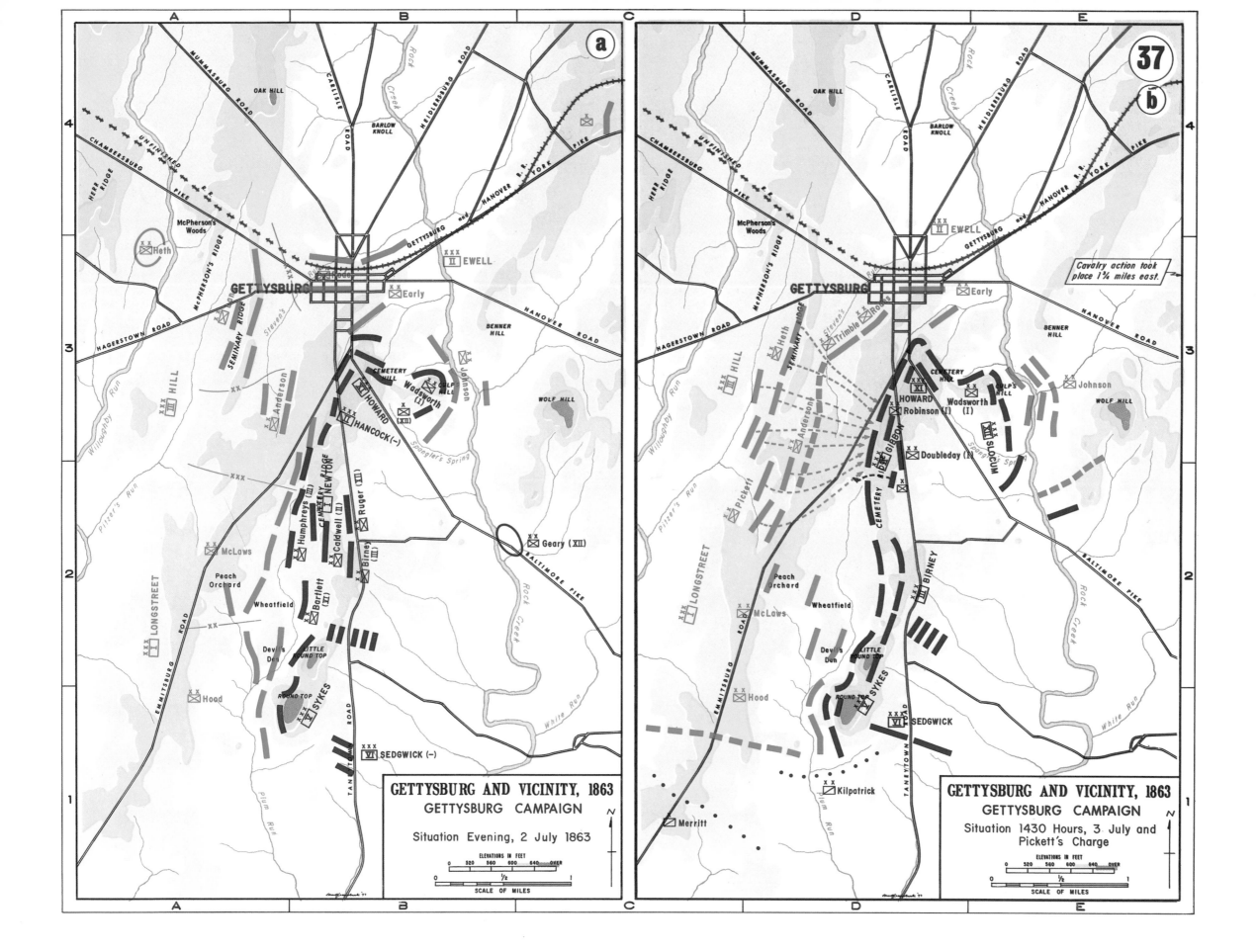

GETTYSBURG AND VICINITY, 1863
GETTYSBURG CAMPAIGN

Situation Evening, 2 July 1863

ELEVATIONS IN FEET
520   560   600   640   OVER

0   ½   1
SCALE OF MILES

GETTYSBURG AND VICINITY, 1863
GETTYSBURG CAMPAIGN

Situation 1430 Hours, 3 July and
Pickett's Charge

ELEVATIONS IN FEET
520   560   600   640   OVER

0   ½   1
SCALE OF MILES

Cavalry action took place 1¼ miles east.

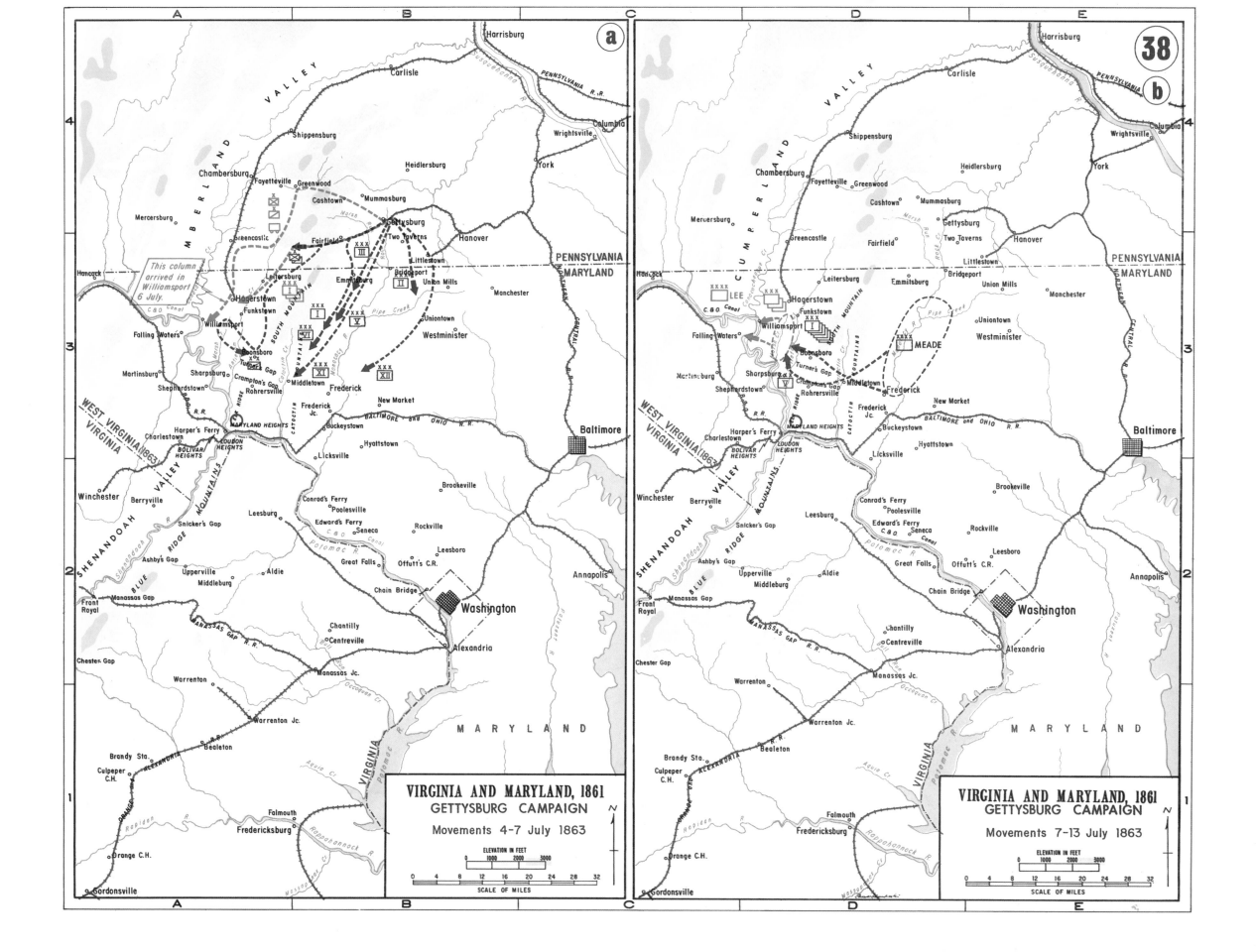

VIRGINIA AND MARYLAND, 1861
GETTYSBURG CAMPAIGN

Movements 4-7 July 1863

ELEVATION IN FEET

1000 2000 3000

0 4 8 12 16 20 24 28 32

SCALE OF MILES

VIRGINIA AND MARYLAND, 1861
GETTYSBURG CAMPAIGN

Movements 7-13 July 1863

ELEVATION IN FEET

1000 2000 3000

0 4 8 12 16 20 24 28 32

SCALE OF MILES

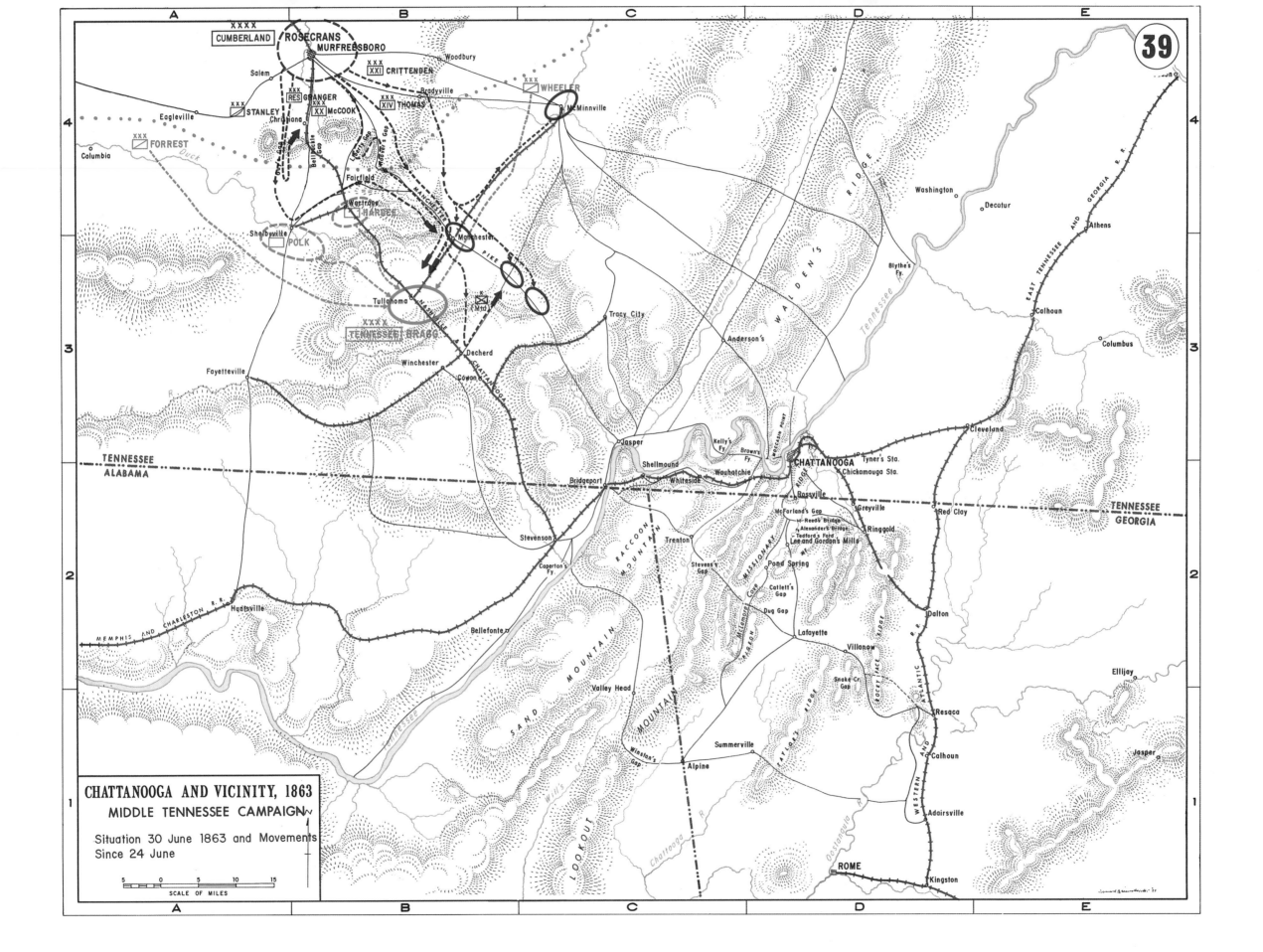

CHATTANOOGA AND VICINITY, 1863
MIDDLE TENNESSEE CAMPAIGN

Situation 30 June 1863 and Movements
Since 24 June

SCALE OF MILES
5   0   5   10   15

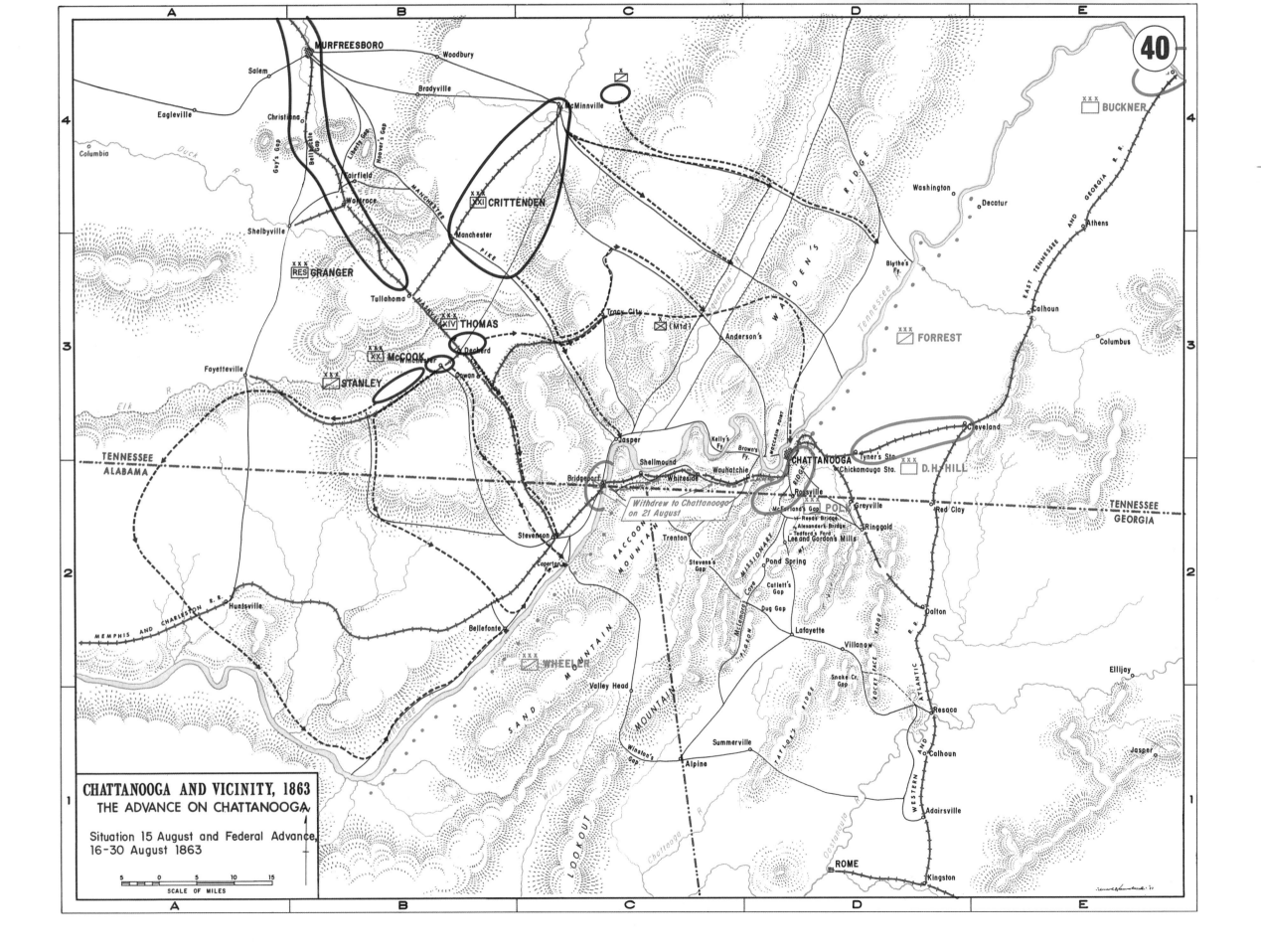

CHATTANOOGA AND VICINITY, 1863
THE ADVANCE ON CHATTANOOGA

Situation 15 August and Federal Advance,
16-30 August 1863

SCALE OF MILES
5   0   5   10   15

Withdrew to Chattanooga
on 21 August

BUCKNER

FORREST

D.H. HILL

POLK

WHEELER

CRITTENDEN

GRANGER

THOMAS

McCOOK

STANLEY

TENNESSEE
ALABAMA

TENNESSEE
GEORGIA

MURFREESBORO

CHATTANOOGA

ROME

Columbia

Eagleville

Salem

Christiana

Fairfield

Wartrace

Shelbyville

Fayetteville

Tullahoma

Decherd

Winchester

Cowan

Woodbury

Bradyville

Guy's Gap

Bell Buckle Gap

Liberty Gap

Hoover's Gap

MANCHESTER PIKE

Manchester

McMinnville

Tracy City

Anderson's

Jasper

Shellmound

Bridgeport

Whiteside

Stevenson

Coperton

Huntsville

MEMPHIS AND CHARLESTON R.R.

Bellefonte

Valley Head

Winston's Gap

Alpine

Summerville

SAND MOUNTAIN

LOOKOUT MOUNTAIN

RACCOON MOUNTAIN

Trenton

Stevens's Gap

Catlett's Gap

Dug Gap

Lafayette

Villanow

Snake Cr. Gap

Resaca

Calhoun

Adairsville

Kingston

Kelly's Fy.

Brown's Fy.

MOCCASIN POINT

WALDEN'S RIDGE

MISSIONARY RIDGE

Wauhatchie

Rossville

McFarland's Gap

Reed's Bridge

Alexander's Bridge

Tedford's Ford

Lee and Gordon's Mills

Pond Spring

Tyner's Sta.

Chickamauga Sta.

Greyville

Ringgold

Red Clay

Dalton

Washington

Decatur

Athens

Calhoun

Columbus

Cleveland

Blythe's Fy.

Ellijay

Jasper

EAST TENNESSEE AND GEORGIA R.R.

WESTERN AND ATLANTIC R.R.

Duck R.

Elk R.

Tennessee R.

(Mtd)

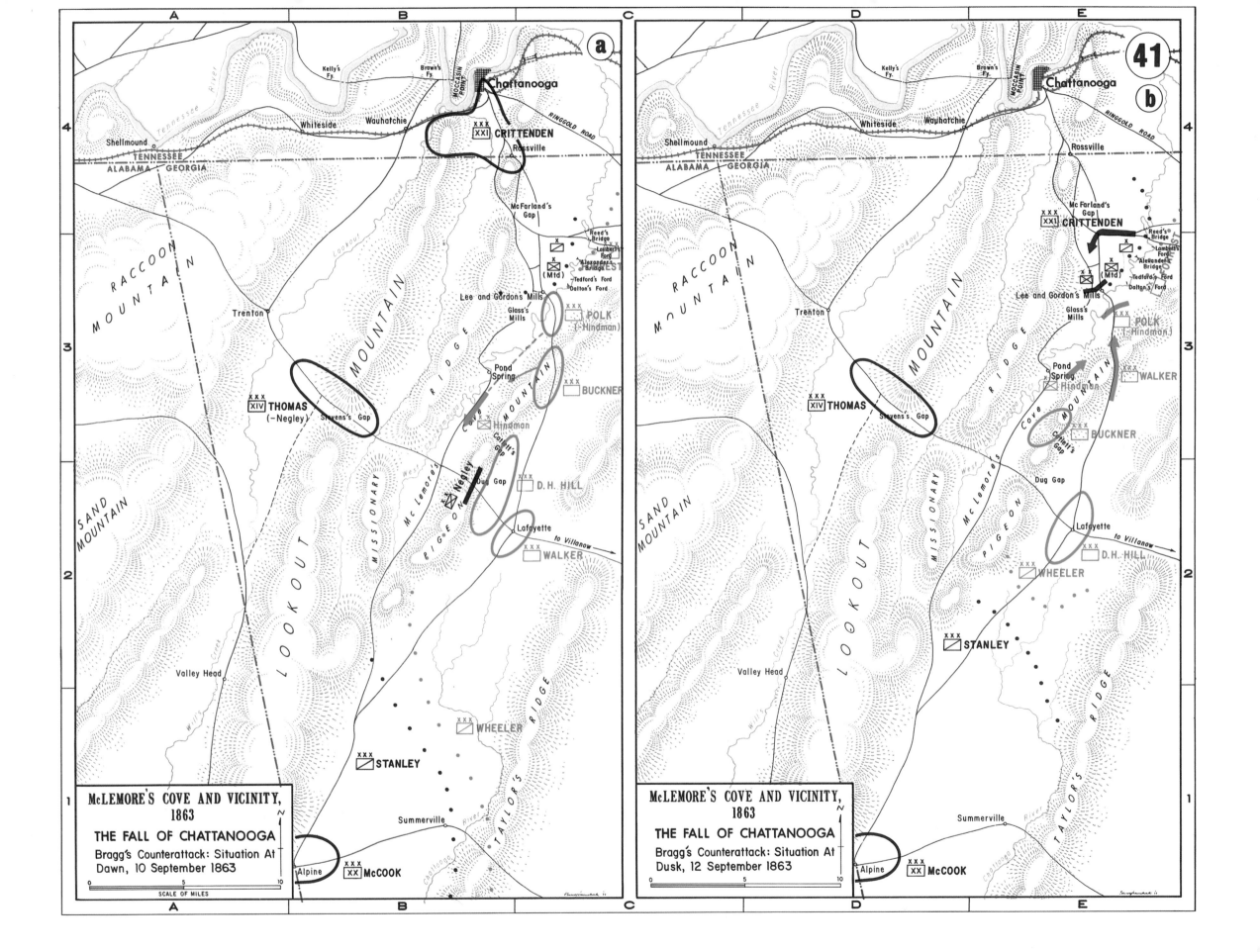

a

Kelly's Fy.
Brown's Fy.
MOCCASIN POINT
Chattanooga
Shellmound
Whiteside
Wauhatchie
RINGGOLD ROAD
TENNESSEE
ALABAMA · GEORGIA
XXX
XXI CRITTENDEN
Rossville
McFarland's Gap
RACCOON MOUNTAIN
Reed's Bridge
Lambert's Ford
Alexander's Bridge
(Mtd)
Trenton
Lee and Gordon's Mills
Glass's Mills
XXX
POLK
(-Hindman)
XXX
XIV THOMAS
(-Negley)
Steven's Gap
Pond Spring
XXX
BUCKNER
LOOKOUT MOUNTAIN
MISSIONARY RIDGE
PIGEON MOUNTAIN
McLemore's Cove
West Chickamauga Creek
Hindman
Catlett's Gap
Negley
Dug Gap
XXX
D. H. HILL
SAND MOUNTAIN
Lafayette
to Villanow
XXX
WALKER
Valley Head
Will's Creek
TAYLOR'S RIDGE
Summerville
Chattooga River
XXX
WHEELER
XXX
STANLEY
Alpine
XXX
XX McCOOK

McLEMORE'S COVE AND VICINITY, 1863
THE FALL OF CHATTANOOGA
Bragg's Counterattack: Situation At Dawn, 10 September 1863

0   5   10
SCALE OF MILES

b

41

Kelly's Fy.
Brown's Fy.
MOCCASIN POINT
Chattanooga
Shellmound
Whiteside
Wauhatchie
RINGGOLD ROAD
TENNESSEE
ALABAMA · GEORGIA
Rossville
McFarland's Gap
XXX
XXI CRITTENDEN
RACCOON MOUNTAIN
Reed's Bridge
Lambert's Ford
Alexander's Bridge
Tedford's Ford
Dalton's Ford
(Mtd)
Trenton
Lee and Gordon's Mills
Glass's Mills
XXX
POLK
(-Hindman)
XXX
XIV THOMAS
Steven's Gap
Pond Spring
Hindman
XXX
WALKER
XXX
BUCKNER
LOOKOUT MOUNTAIN
MISSIONARY RIDGE
PIGEON MOUNTAIN
McLemore's Cove
West Chickamauga Creek
Catlett's Gap
Dug Gap
XXX
D. H. HILL
SAND MOUNTAIN
Lafayette
to Villanow
XXX
WHEELER
Valley Head
Will's Creek
TAYLOR'S RIDGE
XXX
STANLEY
Summerville
Chattooga River
Alpine
XXX
XX McCOOK

McLEMORE'S COVE AND VICINITY, 1863
THE FALL OF CHATTANOOGA
Bragg's Counterattack: Situation At Dusk, 12 September 1863

0   5   10

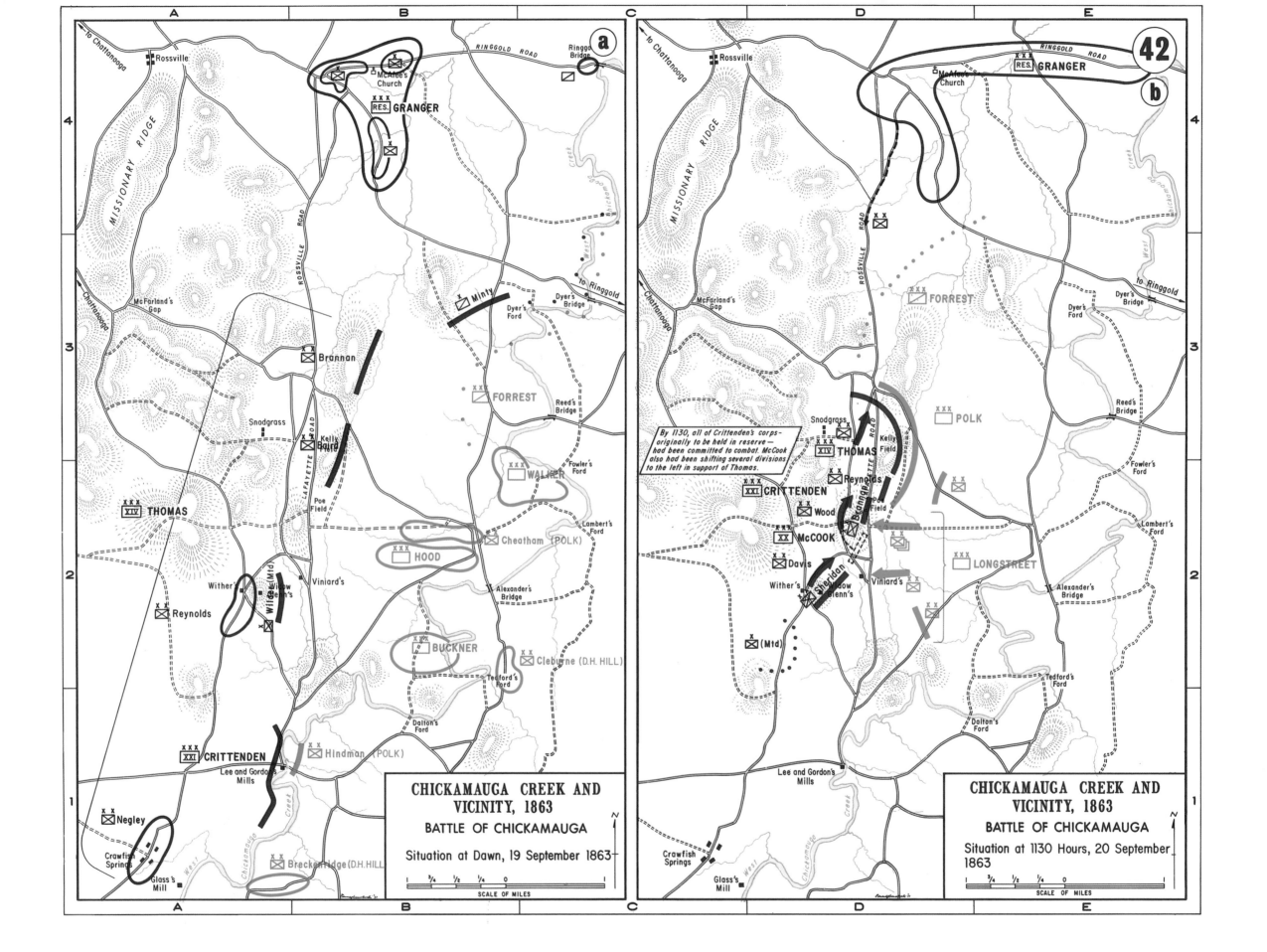

Map a (left panel):

to Chattanooga · Rossville · Missionary Ridge · RINGGOLD ROAD · Ringgold Bridge · McAfee's Church · **a**

RES. **GRANGER**

ROSSVILLE ROAD

McFarland's Gap · Chattanooga · Minty · Dyer's Ford · Dyer's Bridge · to Ringgold

Brannan

LAFAYETTE ROAD · Snodgrass · Kelly's · Baird · **FORREST** · Reed's Bridge

XIV **THOMAS** · Poe Field · **WALKER** · Fowler's Ford

Wither's (Mtd) · Widow Glenn's · Viniard's · Cheatham (POLK) · Lambert's Ford

HOOD

Reynolds · Wilder · Alexander's Bridge

BUCKNER · Cleburne (D.H. HILL) · Tedford's Ford

XXX XXI **CRITTENDEN** · Hindman (POLK)

Lee and Gordon's Mills · Dalton's Ford

Negley

Crawfish Springs · West Chickamauga Creek · Breckenridge (D.H. HILL)

Glass's Mill

CHICKAMAUGA CREEK AND
VICINITY, 1863
BATTLE OF CHICKAMAUGA
Situation at Dawn, 19 September 1863

SCALE OF MILES

Map b (right panel):

42

to Chattanooga · Rossville · RINGGOLD ROAD · RES. **GRANGER** · McAfee's Church · **b**

Missionary Ridge · ROSSVILLE ROAD

FORREST · Dyer's Bridge · to Ringgold

McFarland's Gap · Chattanooga · Reed's Bridge · Fowler's Ford

By 1130, all of Crittenden's corps—
originally to be held in reserve—
had been committed to combat. McCook
also had been shifting several divisions
to the left in support of Thomas.

Snodgrass · XIV **THOMAS** · Kelly Field · **POLK**

Reynolds · Poe Field

XXX **CRITTENDEN** · Brannon · Lambert's Ford

Wood

XX **McCOOK** · **LONGSTREET**

Davis · Sheridan · Alexander's Bridge

Wither's · Widow Glenn's · Viniard's

(Mtd)

Lee and Gordon's Mills · Dalton's Ford

Crawfish Springs · West Chickamauga Creek · Tedford's Ford

Glass's Mill

CHICKAMAUGA CREEK AND
VICINITY, 1863
BATTLE OF CHICKAMAUGA
Situation at 1130 Hours, 20 September
1863

SCALE OF MILES

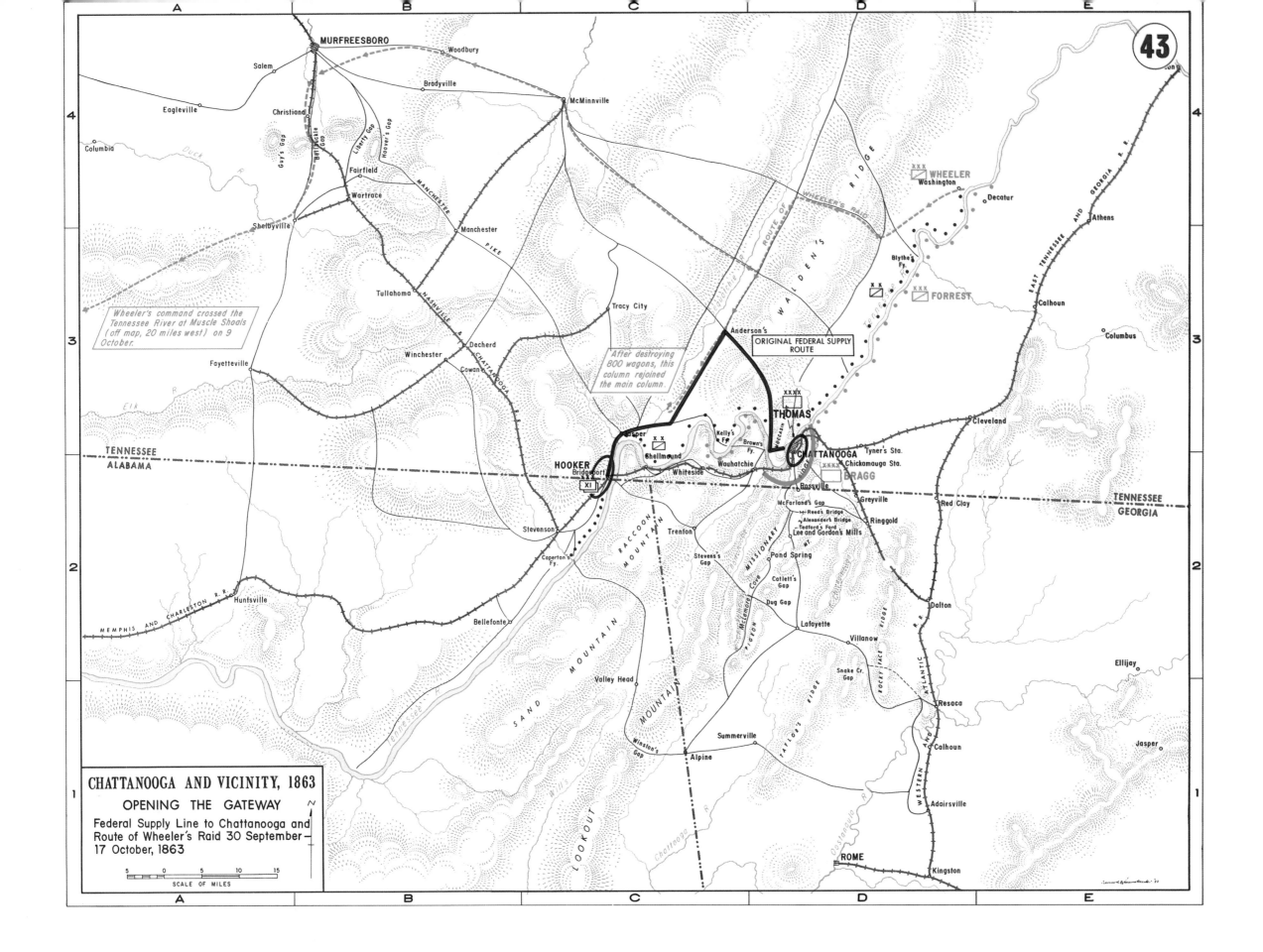

CHATTANOOGA AND VICINITY, 1863

OPENING THE GATEWAY

Federal Supply Line to Chattanooga and Route of Wheeler's Raid 30 September — 17 October, 1863

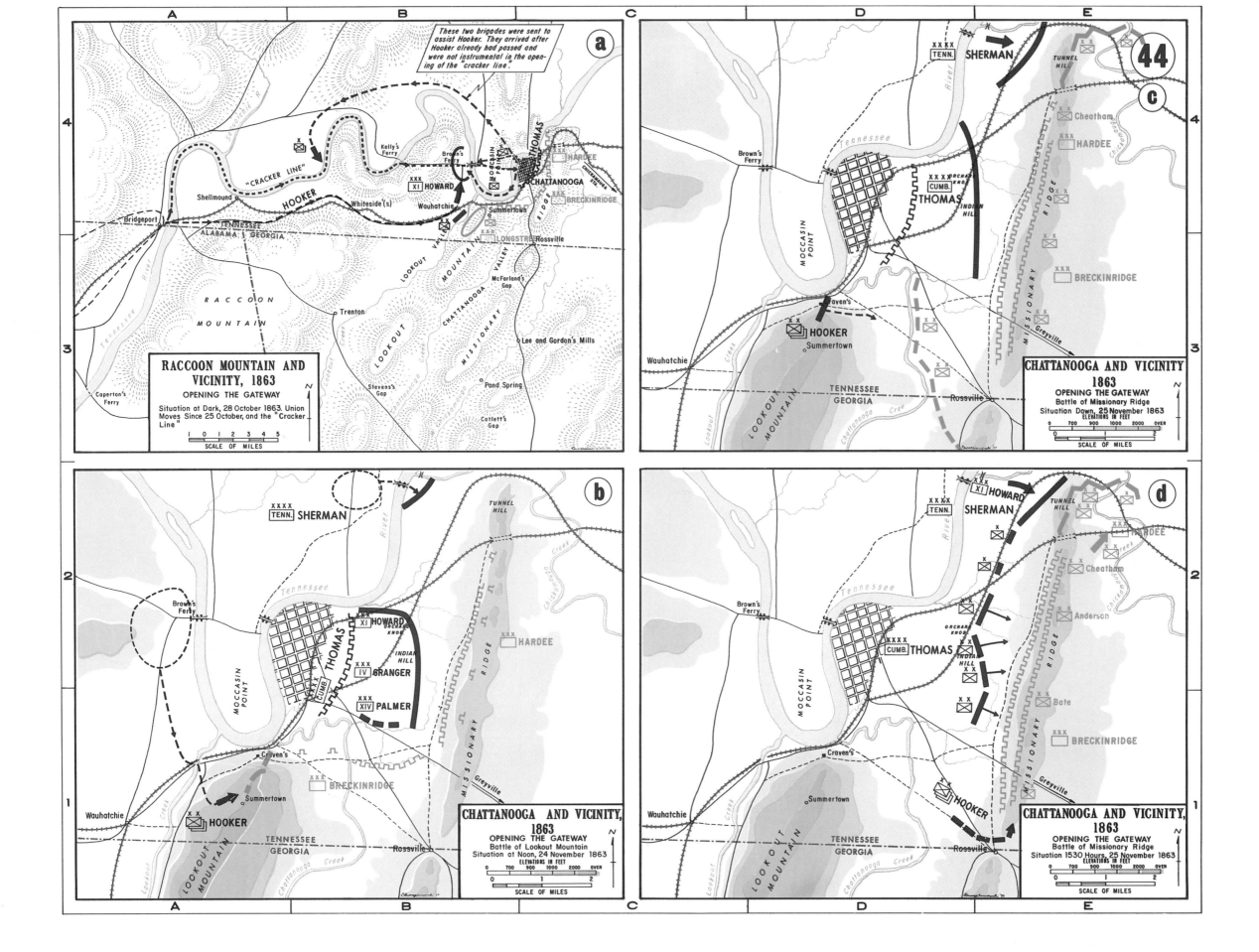

a

These two brigades were sent to assist Hooker. They arrived after Hooker already had passed and were not instrumental in the opening of the "cracker line".

"CRACKER LINE"

Kelly's Ferry

Brown's Ferry

MOCCASIN POINT

THOMAS

HARDEE

CHATTANOOGA

BRECKINRIDGE

XXX XI HOWARD

HOOKER

Shellmound

Whiteside(s)

Wauhatchie

Summertown

LONGSTREET

Rossville

Bridgeport

TENNESSEE
ALABAMA | GEORGIA

RACCOON MOUNTAIN

LOOKOUT MOUNTAIN

LOOKOUT VALLEY

CHATTANOOGA VALLEY

MISSIONARY

McFarland's Gap

Trenton

Lee and Gordon's Mills

Caperton's Ferry

Stevens's Gap

Pond Spring

Catlett's Gap

RACCOON MOUNTAIN AND VICINITY, 1863
OPENING THE GATEWAY
Situation at Dark, 28 October 1863. Union Moves Since 25 October, and the "Cracker Line"

SCALE OF MILES
1 0 1 2 3 4 5

c

44

XXXX TENN.

SHERMAN

TUNNEL HILL

Cheatham

HARDEE

Brown's Ferry

XXXX CUMB.

THOMAS

ORCHARD KNOB

INDIAN HILL

BRECKINRIDGE

MISSIONARY RIDGE

HOOKER

Summertown

Craven's

Wauhatchie

TENNESSEE
GEORGIA

Rossville

Greyville

CHATTANOOGA AND VICINITY 1863
OPENING THE GATEWAY
Battle of Missionary Ridge
Situation Dawn, 25 November 1863
ELEVATIONS IN FEET
0 700 900 2000 OVER

SCALE OF MILES
0 1 2

b

XXXX TENN. SHERMAN

TUNNEL HILL

Brown's Ferry

XXX XI HOWARD
ORCHARD KNOB

THOMAS

XXX CUMB.

INDIAN HILL

XXX IV GRANGER

XXX XIV PALMER

HARDEE

MISSIONARY RIDGE

Craven's

BRECKINRIDGE

HOOKER

Summertown

Wauhatchie

TENNESSEE
GEORGIA

Rossville

Greyville

CHATTANOOGA AND VICINITY, 1863
OPENING THE GATEWAY
Battle of Lookout Mountain
Situation at Noon, 24 November 1863
ELEVATIONS IN FEET
0 700 900 1000 2000 OVER

SCALE OF MILES
0 1 2

d

XXXX TENN.
XXX XI HOWARD

SHERMAN

TUNNEL HILL

HARDEE

Brown's Ferry

Cheatham

Anderson

XXXX CUMB.

THOMAS

ORCHARD KNOB

INDIAN HILL

Bate

MISSIONARY RIDGE

BRECKINRIDGE

HOOKER

Craven's

Summertown

Wauhatchie

MOCCASIN POINT

TENNESSEE
GEORGIA

Rossville

Greyville

CHATTANOOGA AND VICINITY, 1863
OPENING THE GATEWAY
Battle of Missionary Ridge
Situation 1530 Hours, 25 November 1863
ELEVATIONS IN FEET
0 700 900 2000 OVER

SCALE OF MILES
0 1 2

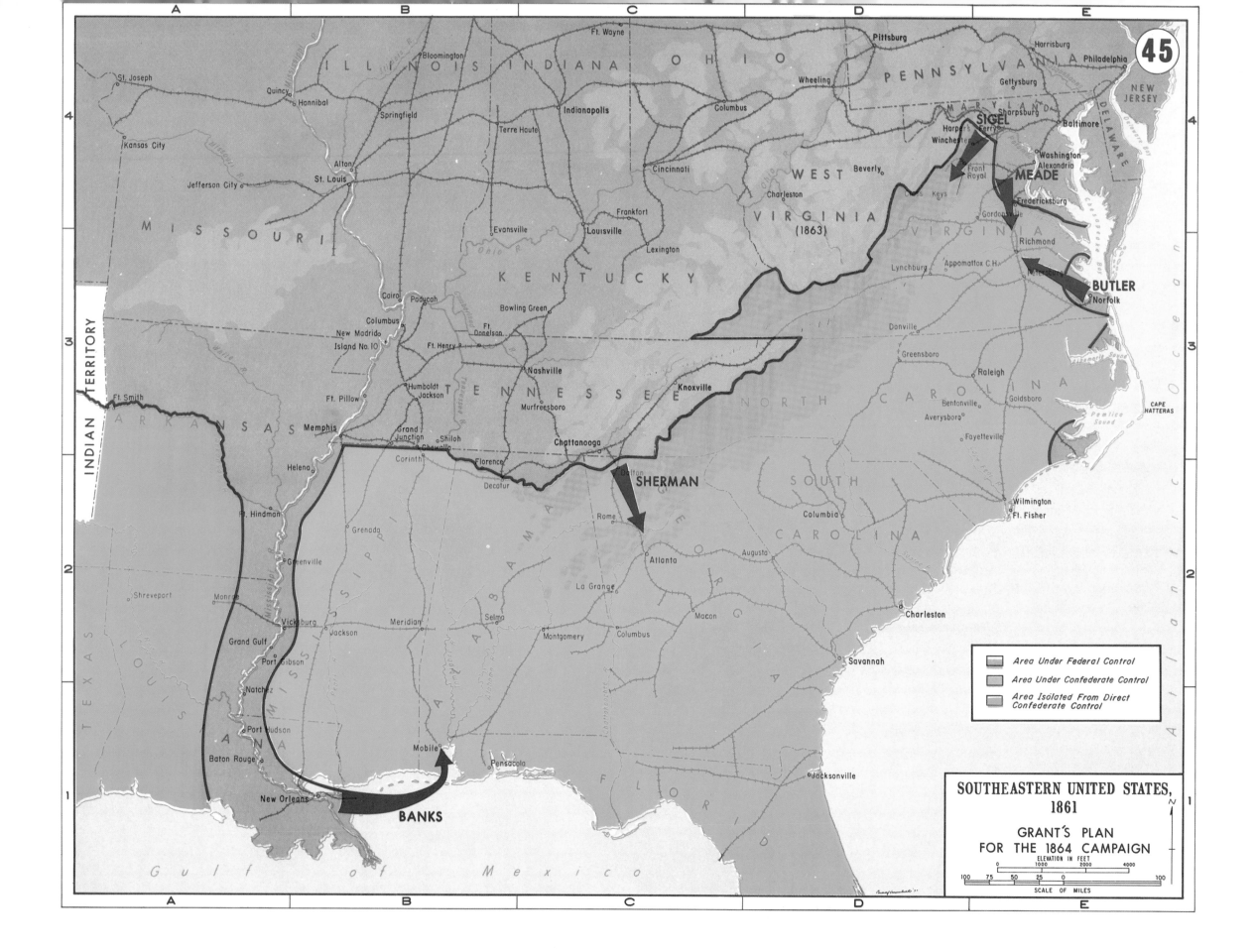

SOUTHEASTERN UNITED STATES,
1861

GRANT'S PLAN
FOR THE 1864 CAMPAIGN

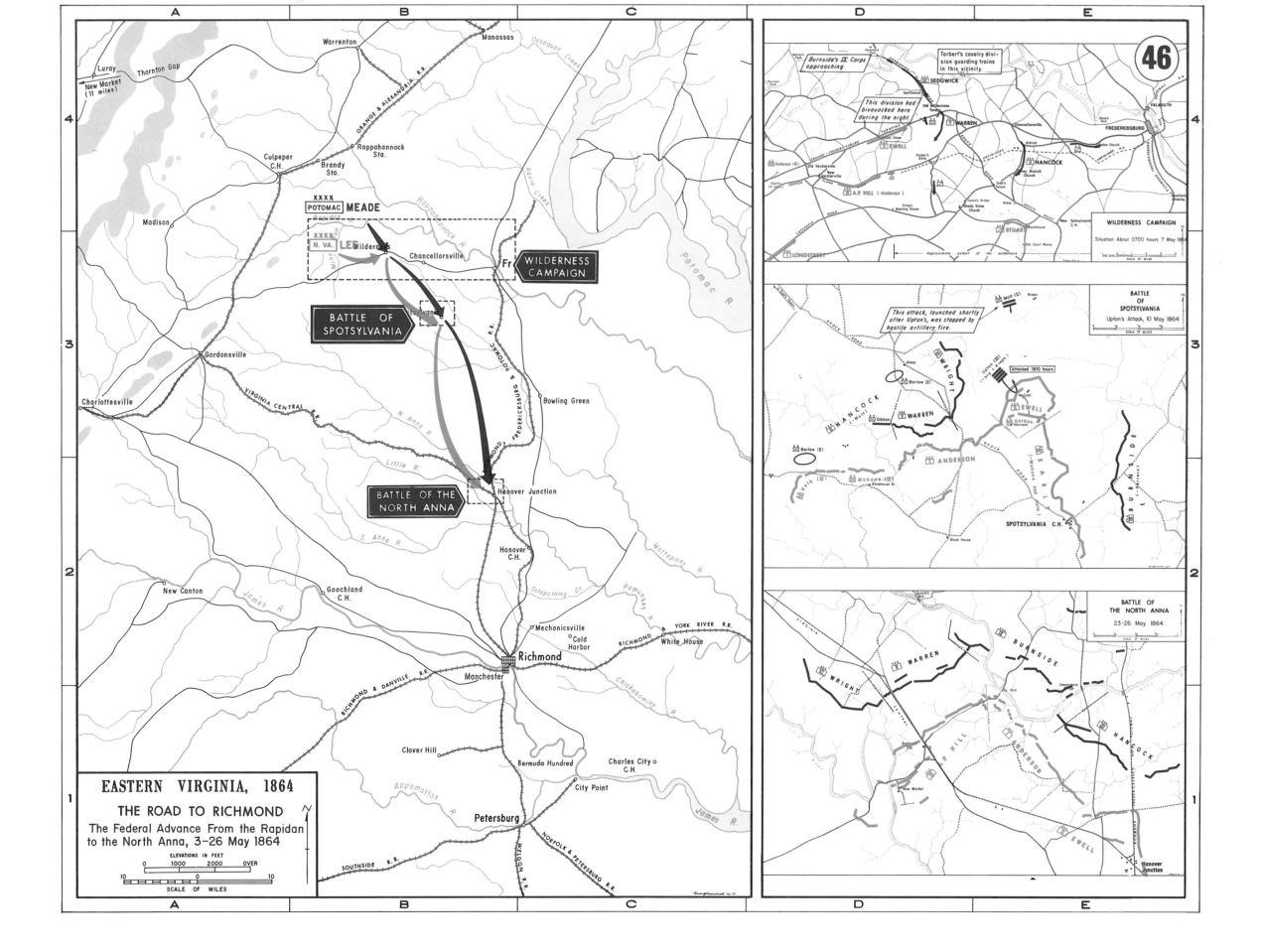

EASTERN VIRGINIA, 1864

THE ROAD TO RICHMOND

The Federal Advance From the Rapidan
to the North Anna, 3–26 May 1864

ELEVATIONS IN FEET
0   1000   2000   OVER

SCALE OF MILES

WILDERNESS CAMPAIGN

BATTLE OF SPOTSYLVANIA

BATTLE OF THE NORTH ANNA

XXXX POTOMAC MEADE

XXXX N. VA. LEE

46

WILDERNESS CAMPAIGN
Situation About 0700 hours 7 May 1864

Burnside's IX Corps approaching.

Torbert's cavalry division guarding trains in this vicinity.

This division had bivouacked here during the night.

BATTLE OF SPOTSYLVANIA
Upton's Attack, 10 May 1864

This attack, launched shortly after Upton's, was stopped by hostile artillery fire.

Attacked 1810 hours

BATTLE OF THE NORTH ANNA
23–26 May 1864

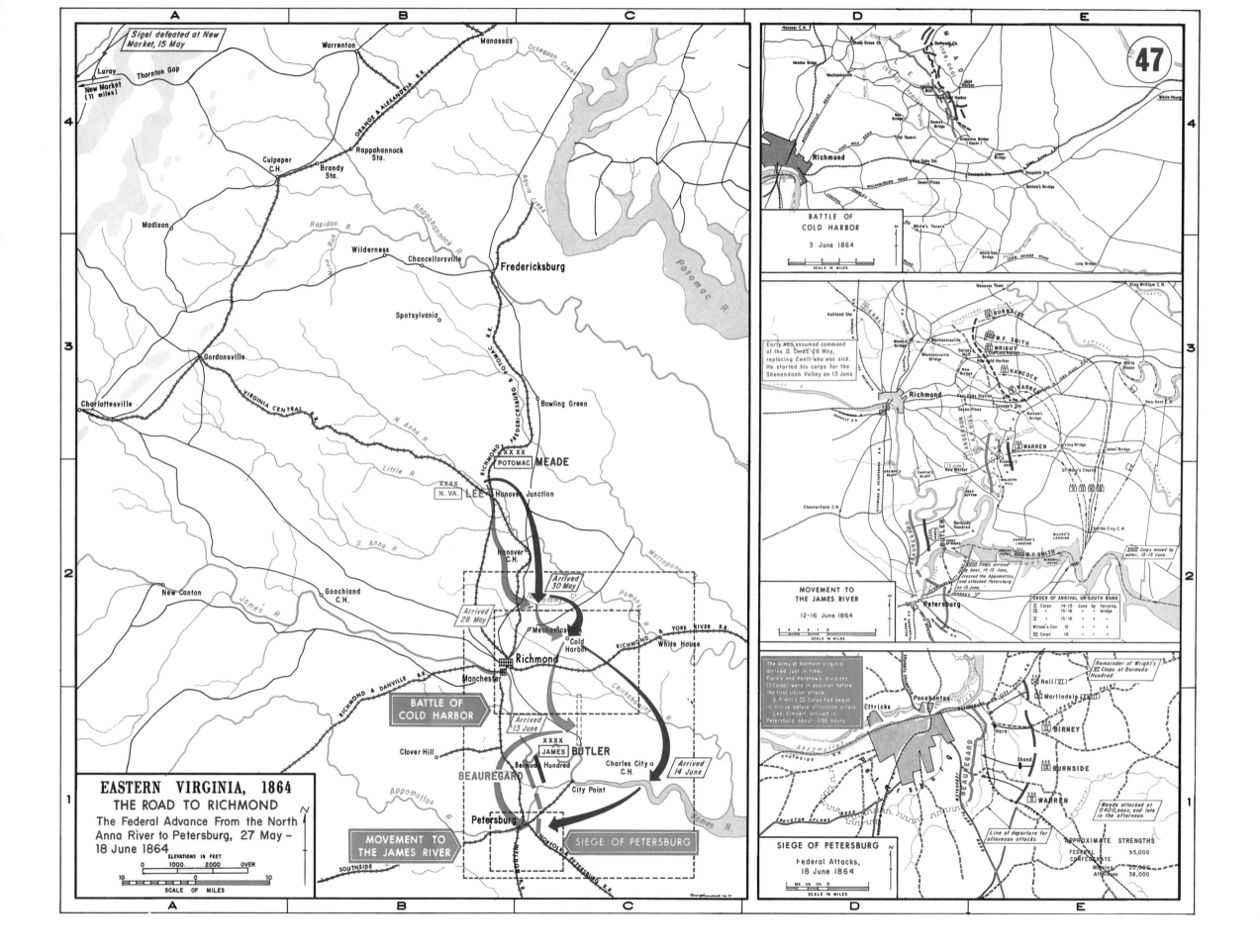

Sigel defeated at New Market, 15 May

Luray
New Market (11 miles)
Thornton Gap
Warrenton
Manassas
Occoquan Creek
Culpeper C.H.
Rappahannock Sta.
Brandy Sta.
Madison
Rapidan R.
Wilderness
Chancellorsville
Fredericksburg
Potomac R.
Gordonsville
Spotsylvania
Charlottesville
VIRGINIA CENTRAL R.R.
N. Anna R.
Bowling Green
Little R.
RICHMOND FREDERICKSBURG & POTOMAC R.R.
XXXX POTOMAC MEADE
XXXX N. VA. LEE Hanover Junction
S. Anna R.
New Canton
Goochland C.H.
James R.
Hanover C.H.
Arrived 30 May
Arrived 28 May
Mechanicsville
Cold Harbor
Richmond
RICHMOND & YORK RIVER R.R.
White House
Chickahominy R.
Mattapony R.
Pamunkey R.
Manchester
RICHMOND & DANVILLE R.R.
BATTLE OF COLD HARBOR
Arrived 13 June
Clover Hill
XXXX JAMES BUTLER
BEAUREGARD
Bermuda Hundred
City Point
Charles City C.H.
Arrived 14 June
Appomattox R.
Petersburg
MOVEMENT TO THE JAMES RIVER
SIEGE OF PETERSBURG
SOUTHSIDE
NORFOLK & PETERSBURG R.R.

EASTERN VIRGINIA, 1864
THE ROAD TO RICHMOND
The Federal Advance From the North Anna River to Petersburg, 27 May – 18 June 1864

ELEVATIONS IN FEET
1000   2000   OVER
10   0   10
SCALE OF MILES

47

Hanover C.H.
Shady Grove Ch.
Bethesda Ch.
Meadow Bridge
Mechanicsville
Old Harbor
White House
Richmond
Mechanicsville Road
Nine Mile Road
Gaines Mill
Dispatch Sta.
Seven Pines
Bottom's Bridge
White Oak Bridge Road
Long Bridge
BATTLE OF COLD HARBOR
3 June 1864
SCALE IN MILES

Hanover Town
King William C.H.
Ashland Sta.
EARLY
Telegraph Road
BURNSIDE
Meadow Bridge
W.F. SMITH
Mechanicsville
WRIGHT
Gaines Mill
Cold Harbor
HANCOCK
New Cold Harbor
White House
Richmond
Danville R.R.
Fair Oaks Station
Seven Pines
Savage's Sta.
Bottom's Bridge
New Kent C.H.
WARREN
Long Bridge
St. Mary's Church
Chesterfield C.H.
Drewry's Bluff
Chapin's Bluff
New Market
Malvern Hill
DEEP BOTTOM
Wilcox's Landing
Charles City C.H.
BEAUREGARD
Bermuda Hundred
Harrison's Landing
W.F. SMITH
Windmill Point

Early had assumed command of the II Corps 28 May, replacing Ewell who was sick. He started his corps for the Shenandoah Valley on 13 June.

XVIII Corps moved by water, 13-15 June.
XVIII Corps arrived by boat, 14-15 June, crossed the Appomattox, and attacked Petersburg on 15 June.

MOVEMENT TO THE JAMES RIVER
12-16 June 1864

ORDER OF ARRIVAL ON SOUTH BANK		
II Corps	14-15 June	by ferrying
IX "	15-16 "	" bridge
V "	15-16 "	" "
Wilson's Cav.	16 "	" "
VI "	16 "	" "

Petersburg
SCALE IN MILES

The Army of Northern Virginia arrived just in time. Field's and Kershaw's divisions (I Corps) were in position before the first Union attack.
A.P. Hill's III Corps had begun to arrive before afternoon attack. Lee, himself, arrived in Petersburg about 1130 hours.

Remainder of Wright's VI Corps at Bermuda Hundred.
Neill (VI)
Martindale (XVIII)
Pocahontas
Ettricks
BIRNEY
Hare
Shand
BURNSIDE
BEAUREGARD
WARREN
Appomattox R.
SOUTHSIDE R.R.

Meade attacked at 0400, noon, and late in the afternoon.

Line of departure for afternoon attacks.

APPROXIMATE STRENGTHS
FEDERAL   CONFEDERATE
95,000
Morning   20,000
Afternoon   38,000

SIEGE OF PETERSBURG
Federal Attacks, 18 June 1864
SCALE IN MILES

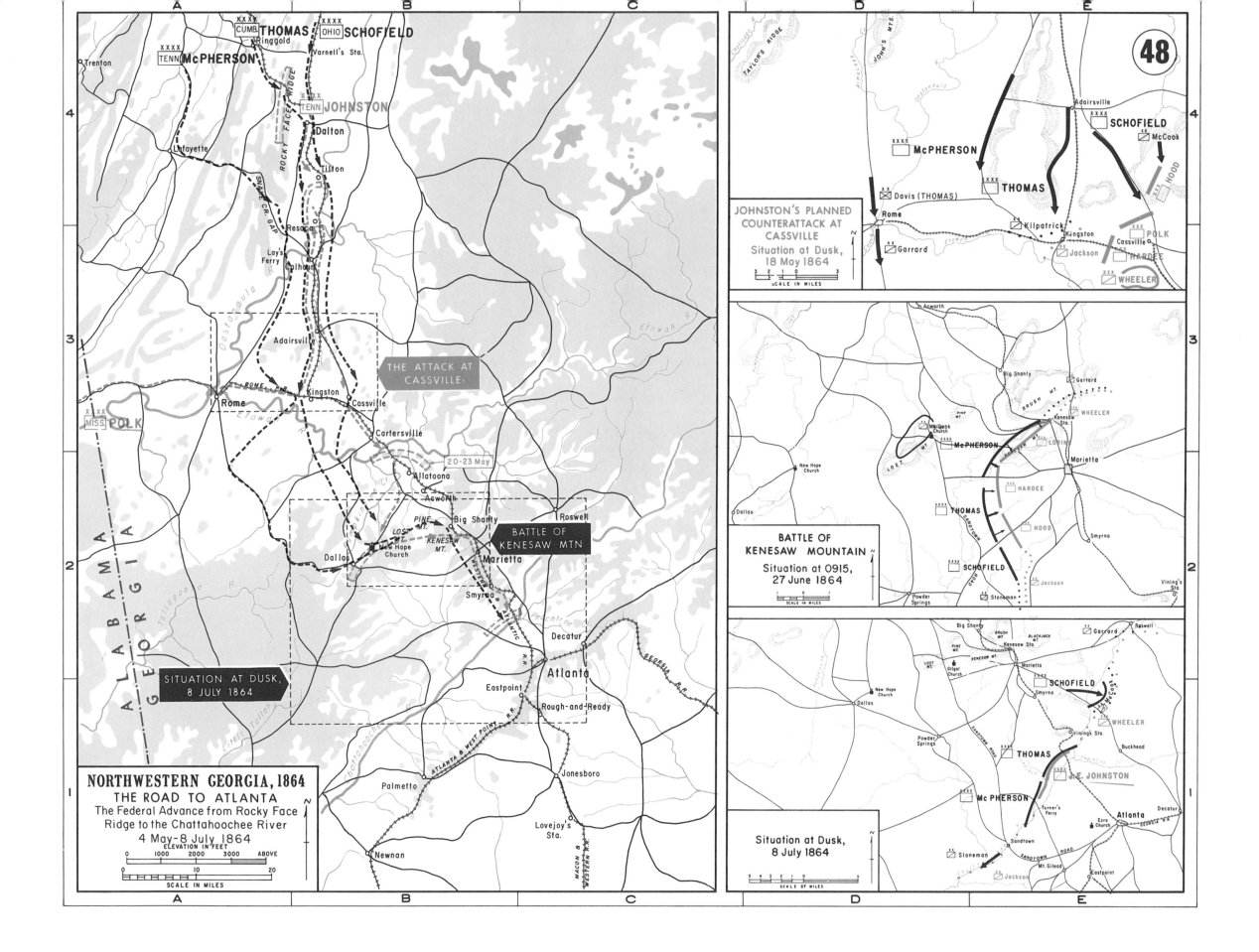

48

JOHNSTON'S PLANNED COUNTERATTACK AT CASSVILLE
Situation at Dusk,
18 May 1864
SCALE IN MILES

BATTLE OF KENESAW MOUNTAIN
Situation at 0915,
27 June 1864
SCALE IN MILES

Situation at Dusk,
8 July 1864
SCALE OF MILES

THE ATTACK AT CASSVILLE

20-23 May

BATTLE OF KENESAW MTN

SITUATION AT DUSK,
8 JULY 1864

NORTHWESTERN GEORGIA, 1864
THE ROAD TO ATLANTA
The Federal Advance from Rocky Face
Ridge to the Chattahoochee River
4 May-8 July 1864
ELEVATION IN FEET
0   1000   2000   3000 ABOVE
0   10   20
SCALE IN MILES

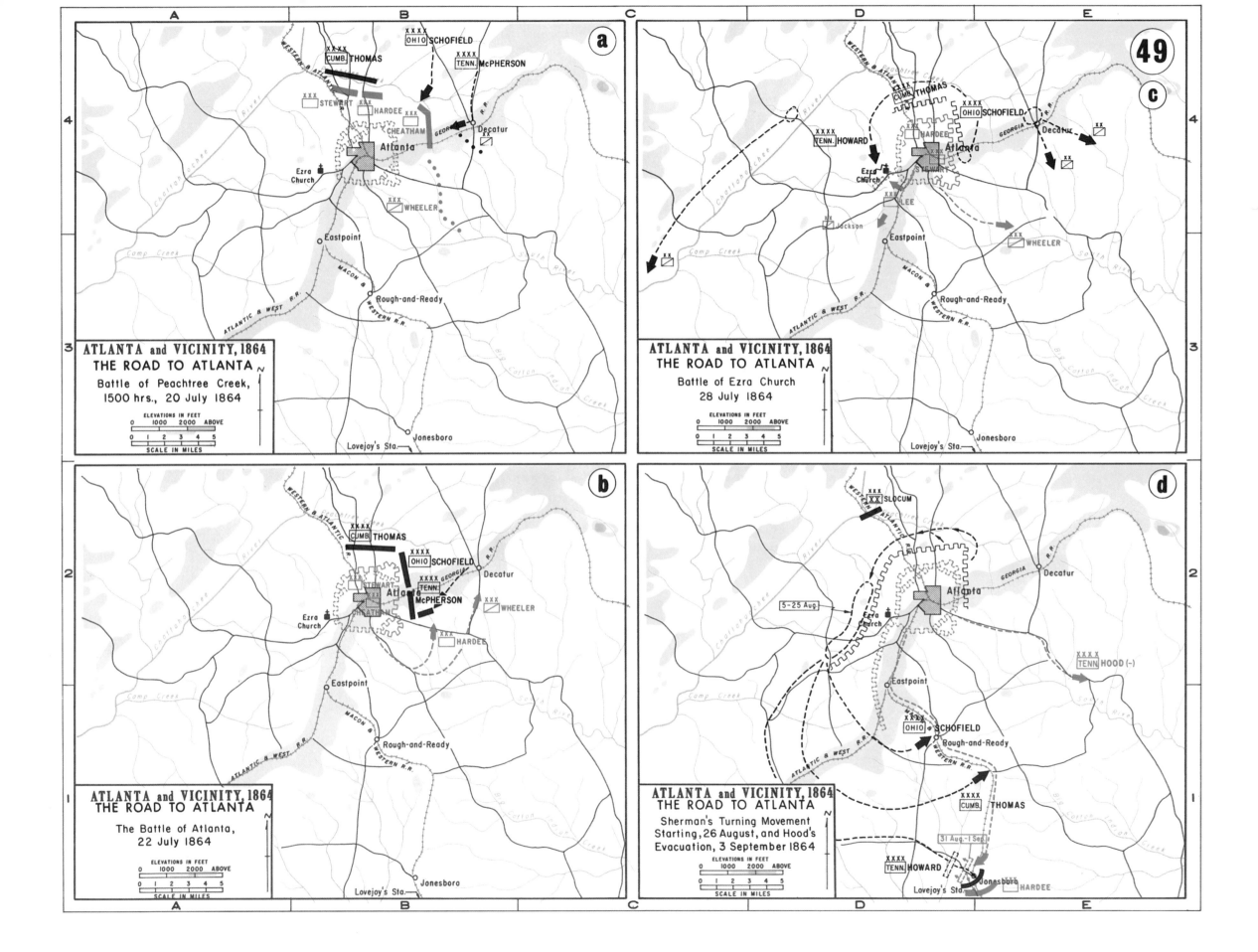

a

ATLANTA and VICINITY, 1864
THE ROAD TO ATLANTA

Battle of Peachtree Creek,
1500 hrs., 20 July 1864

ELEVATIONS IN FEET
0 1000 2000 ABOVE
0 1 2 3 4 5
SCALE IN MILES

b

ATLANTA and VICINITY, 1864
THE ROAD TO ATLANTA

The Battle of Atlanta,
22 July 1864

ELEVATIONS IN FEET
0 1000 2000 ABOVE
0 1 2 3 4 5
SCALE IN MILES

c

49

ATLANTA and VICINITY, 1864
THE ROAD TO ATLANTA

Battle of Ezra Church
28 July 1864

ELEVATIONS IN FEET
0 1000 2000 ABOVE
0 1 2 3 4 5
SCALE IN MILES

d

ATLANTA and VICINITY, 1864
THE ROAD TO ATLANTA

Sherman's Turning Movement
Starting, 26 August, and Hood's
Evacuation, 3 September 1864

ELEVATIONS IN FEET
0 1000 2000 ABOVE
0 1 2 3 4 5
SCALE IN MILES

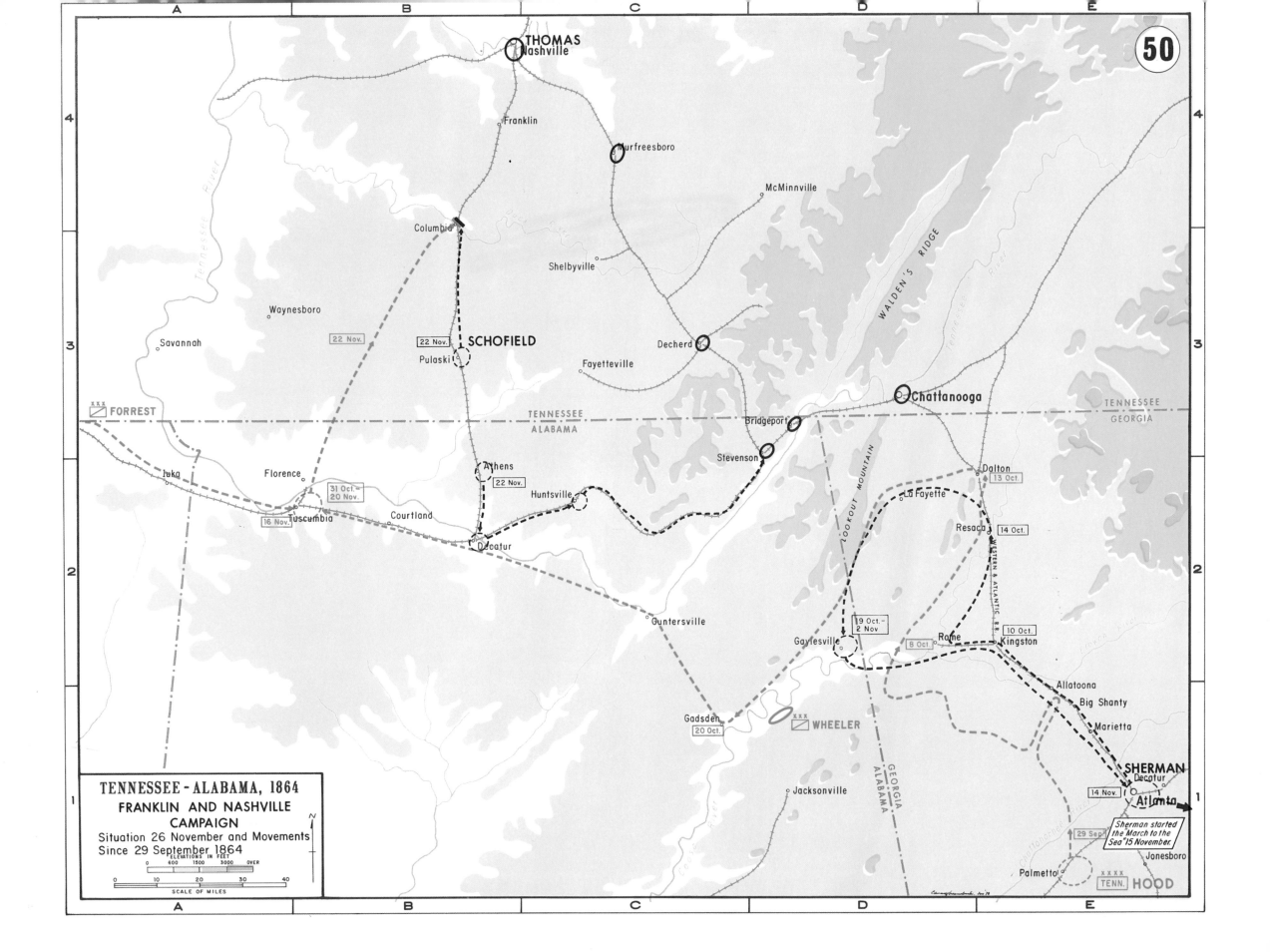

50

TENNESSEE - ALABAMA, 1864
FRANKLIN AND NASHVILLE
CAMPAIGN
Situation 26 November and Movements
Since 29 September 1864

ELEVATIONS IN FEET
600 1500 3000 OVER

0   10   20   30   40
SCALE OF MILES

THOMAS
Nashville

Franklin

Murfreesboro

McMinnville

Columbia

Shelbyville

Waynesboro

22 Nov.   22 Nov.   SCHOFIELD
Savannah   Pulaski
                          Fayetteville   Dechard

FORREST

TENNESSEE   Bridgeport   Chattanooga
ALABAMA   TENNESSEE
                                     GEORGIA

Iuka   Florence   Stevenson
                    Athens   Dalton
                    22 Nov.   13 Oct.
31 Oct.-
20 Nov.   Huntsville   La Fayette
16 Nov. Tuscumbia Courtland   Resaca
                        Decatur   14 Oct.

                                    19 Oct.-   10 Oct.
                                    2 Nov.   Rome
                        Guntersville   8 Oct. Kingston
                                    Gaylesville

                                                Allatoona
                                                Big Shanty

                    Gadsden   Marietta
                    20 Oct.   WHEELER

                                                SHERMAN
                                                Decatur
            Jacksonville   GEORGIA   14 Nov. Atlanta
                                ALABAMA

                                            Sherman started
                                            the March to the
                                            Sea 15 November.

                                            29 Sep
            Palmetto   Jonesboro
                                            TENN. HOOD

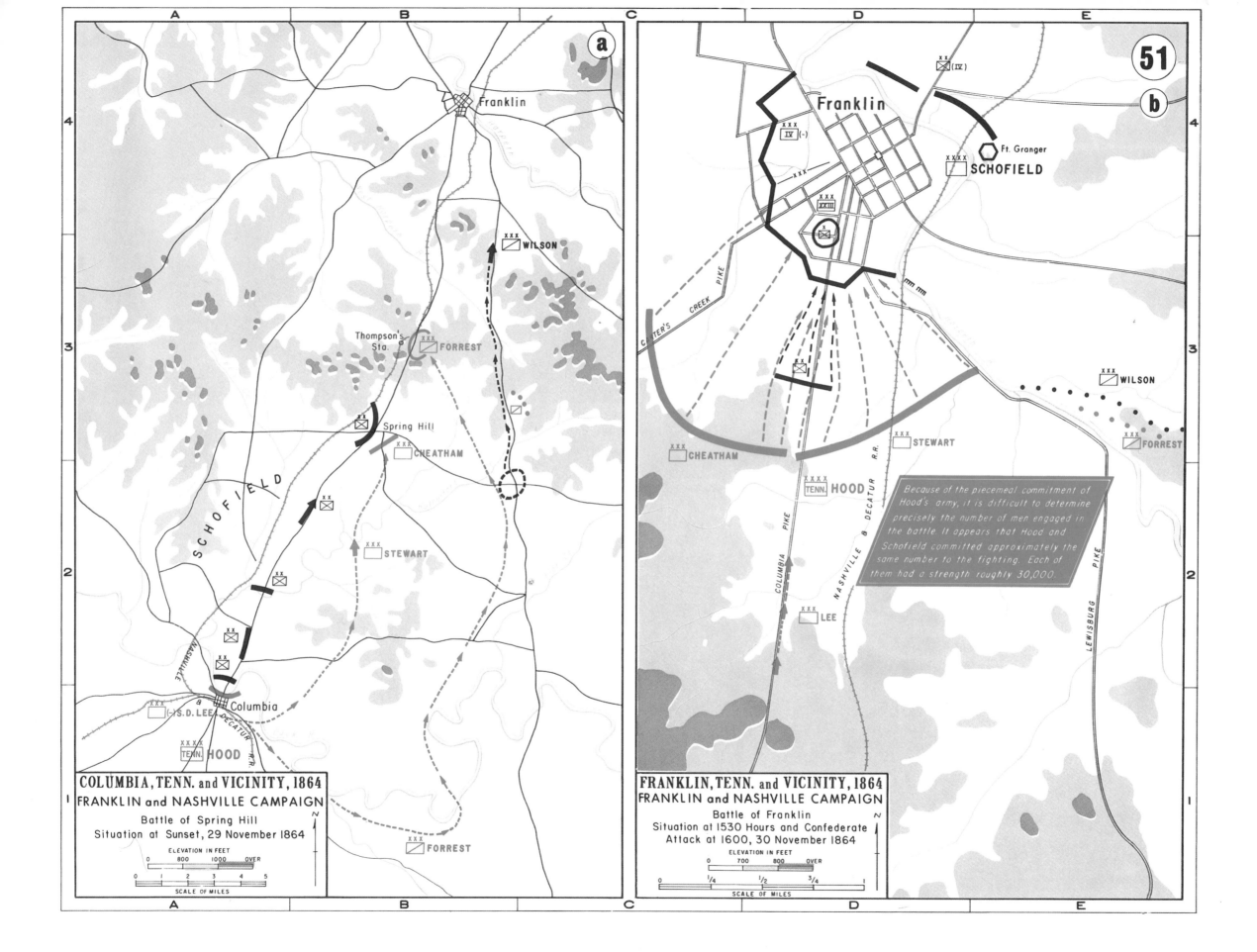

a

Franklin

XXX WILSON

Thompson's Sta. XXX FORREST

XX

Spring Hill

XX

XXX CHEATHAM

SCHOFIELD

XX

XXX STEWART

XX

XX

XX

XXX (-) S.D. LEE   Columbia

XXXX TENN. HOOD

DECATUR R.R.

NASHVILLE

XXX FORREST

COLUMBIA, TENN. and VICINITY, 1864
FRANKLIN and NASHVILLE CAMPAIGN

Battle of Spring Hill
Situation at Sunset, 29 November 1864

ELEVATION IN FEET
0   800   1000   OVER

0   1   2   3   4   5
SCALE OF MILES

N

51

b

XX (IV)

Franklin

XXX IV (-)

XXX

Ft. Granger

XXXX

XXXX SCHOFIELD

XXX

CARTER'S CREEK PIKE

COLUMBIA PIKE

XX

XXX WILSON

XXX STEWART

NASHVILLE & DECATUR R.R.

XXX CHEATHAM

XXXX TENN. HOOD

XXX FORREST

LEWISBURG PIKE

Because of the piecemeal commitment of
Hood's army, it is difficult to determine
precisely the number of men engaged in
the battle. It appears that Hood and
Schofield committed approximately the
same number to the fighting. Each of
them had a strength roughly 30,000.

XXX LEE

FRANKLIN, TENN. and VICINITY, 1864
FRANKLIN and NASHVILLE CAMPAIGN

Battle of Franklin
Situation at 1530 Hours and Confederate
Attack at 1600, 30 November 1864

N

ELEVATION IN FEET
0   700   800   OVER

0   1/4   1/2   3/4   1
SCALE OF MILES

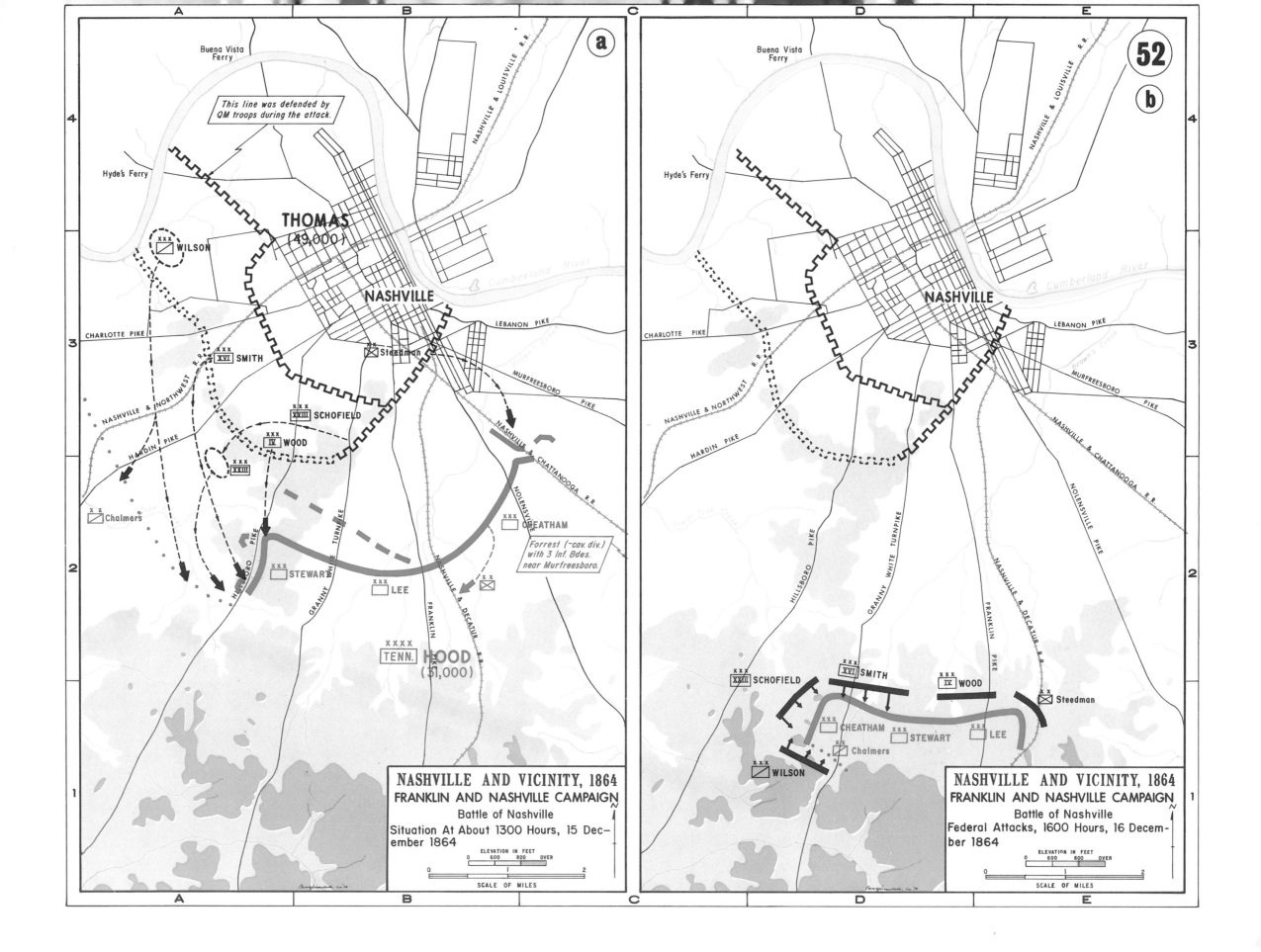

a

Buena Vista Ferry

This line was defended by QM troops during the attack.

NASHVILLE & LOUISVILLE R.R.

Hyde's Ferry

THOMAS
(49,000)

Cumberland River

XXX WILSON

NASHVILLE

CHARLOTTE PIKE

LEBANON PIKE

XVI XXX SMITH

XX Steedman

MURFREESBORO PIKE

NASHVILLE & NORTHWEST R.R.

HARDIN PIKE

XXIII XXX SCHOFIELD

IV XXX WOOD

NASHVILLE & CHATTANOOGA R.R.

XXIII XXX

XX Chalmers

XXX CHEATHAM

NOLENSVILLE PIKE

Forrest (~cav. div.) with 3 Inf. Bdes. near Murfreesboro.

GRANNY WHITE TURNPIKE

XXX STEWART

XXX LEE

FRANKLIN PIKE

NASHVILLE & DECATUR R.R.

XXXX
TENN. **HOOD**
(31,000)

NASHVILLE AND VICINITY, 1864
FRANKLIN AND NASHVILLE CAMPAIGN
Battle of Nashville
Situation At About 1300 Hours, 15 December 1864

ELEVATION IN FEET
600 800 OVER

0 SCALE OF MILES 2

b

52

Buena Vista Ferry

NASHVILLE & LOUISVILLE R.R.

Hyde's Ferry

Cumberland River

NASHVILLE

CHARLOTTE PIKE

LEBANON PIKE

MURFREESBORO PIKE

NASHVILLE & NORTHWEST R.R.

HARDIN PIKE

NASHVILLE & CHATTANOOGA R.R.

HILLSBORO PIKE

GRANNY WHITE TURNPIKE

NOLENSVILLE PIKE

FRANKLIN PIKE

NASHVILLE & DECATUR R.R.

XXIII XXX SCHOFIELD

XVI XXX SMITH

IV XXX WOOD

XX Steedman

XXX CHEATHAM

XXX STEWART

XXX LEE

XX Chalmers

XXX WILSON

NASHVILLE AND VICINITY, 1864
FRANKLIN AND NASHVILLE CAMPAIGN
Battle of Nashville
Federal Attacks, 1600 Hours, 16 December 1864

ELEVATION IN FEET
600 800 OVER

0 SCALE OF MILES 2

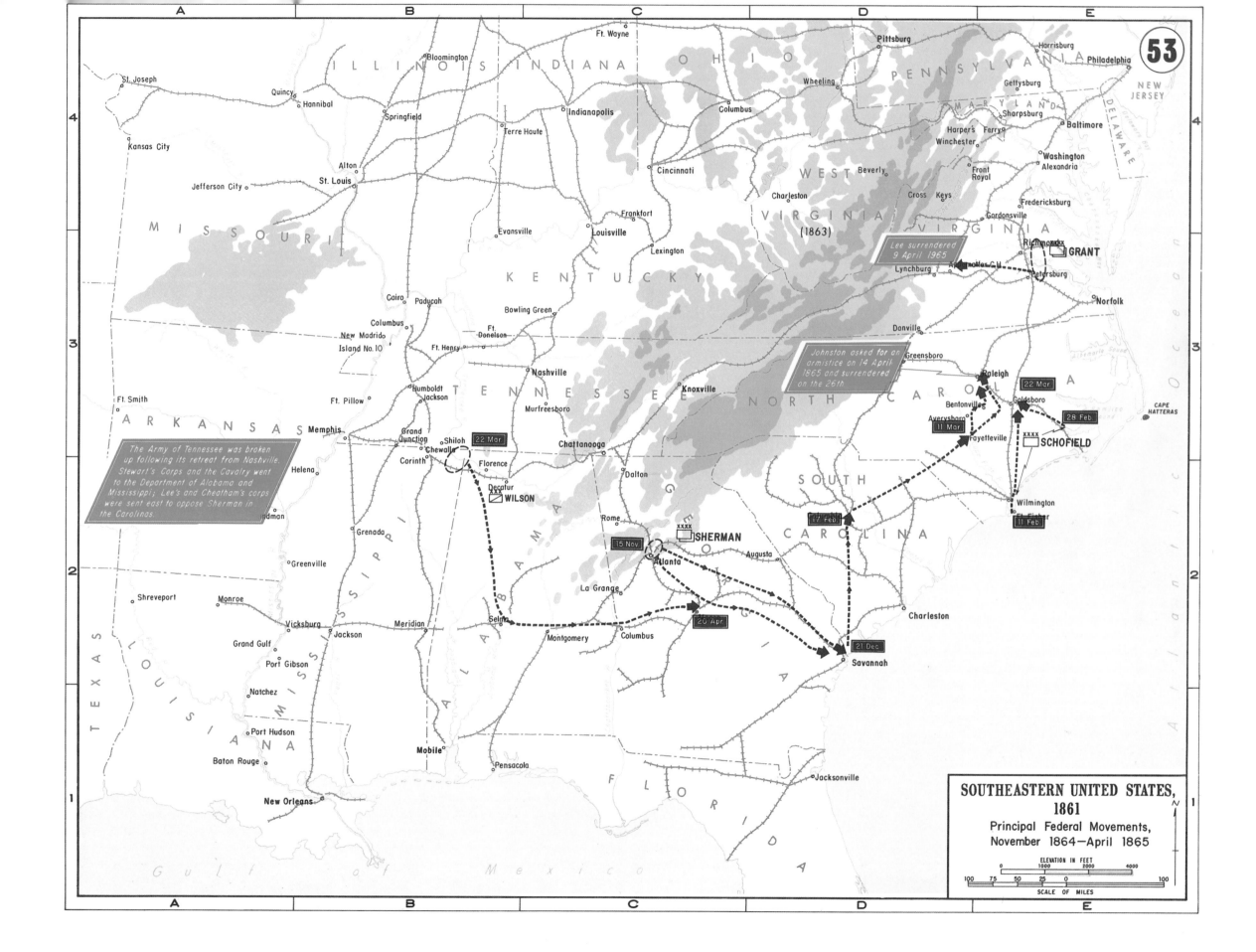

53

The Army of Tennessee was broken up following its retreat from Nashville. Stewart's Corps and the Cavalry went to the Department of Alabama and Mississippi; Lee's and Cheatham's corps were sent east to oppose Sherman in the Carolinas.

Lee surrendered 9 April 1965

Johnston asked for an armistice on 14 April 1865 and surrendered on the 26th.

GRANT

SCHOFIELD

WILSON

SHERMAN

22 Mar

22 Mar

28 Feb.

11 Mar.

11 Feb.

17 Feb.

15 Nov.

20 Apr.

21 Dec.

SOUTHEASTERN UNITED STATES, 1861
Principal Federal Movements,
November 1864–April 1865

ELEVATION IN FEET

SCALE OF MILES

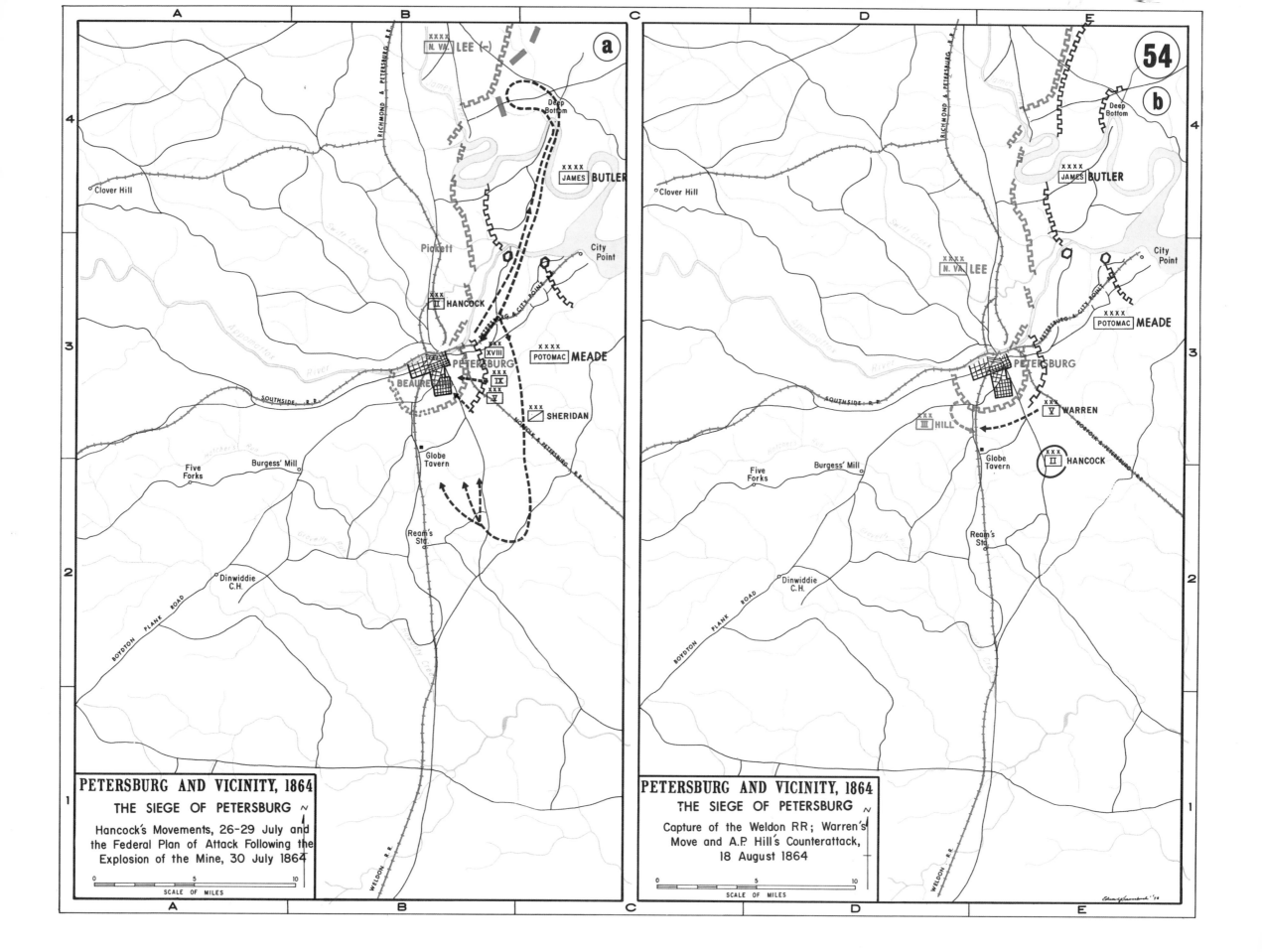

a

XXXX N. VA. LEE (−)

Deep Bottom

XXXX JAMES BUTLER

Clover Hill

City Point

RICHMOND & PETERSBURG R.R.

Pickett

XXX II HANCOCK

XXX XVIII

PETERSBURG

BEAURE

XXX IX

XXX V

XXXX POTOMAC MEADE

XXX SHERIDAN

SOUTHSIDE R.R.

Globe Tavern

Five Forks

Burgess' Mill

Ream's Sta.

Dinwiddie C.H.

BOYDTON PLANK ROAD

WELDON R.R.

54

b

Deep Bottom

XXXX JAMES BUTLER

Clover Hill

XXXX N. VA. LEE

City Point

RICHMOND & PETERSBURG R.R.

PETERSBURG

XXXX POTOMAC MEADE

XXX III HILL

XXX V WARREN

XXX II HANCOCK

SOUTHSIDE R.R.

Globe Tavern

Five Forks

Burgess' Mill

Ream's Sta.

Dinwiddie C.H.

BOYDTON PLANK ROAD

WELDON R.R.

PETERSBURG AND VICINITY, 1864
THE SIEGE OF PETERSBURG ~

Hancock's Movements, 26–29 July and the Federal Plan of Attack Following the Explosion of the Mine, 30 July 1864

0   5   10
SCALE OF MILES

PETERSBURG AND VICINITY, 1864
THE SIEGE OF PETERSBURG ~

Capture of the Weldon RR; Warren's Move and A.P. Hill's Counterattack, 18 August 1864

0   5   10
SCALE OF MILES

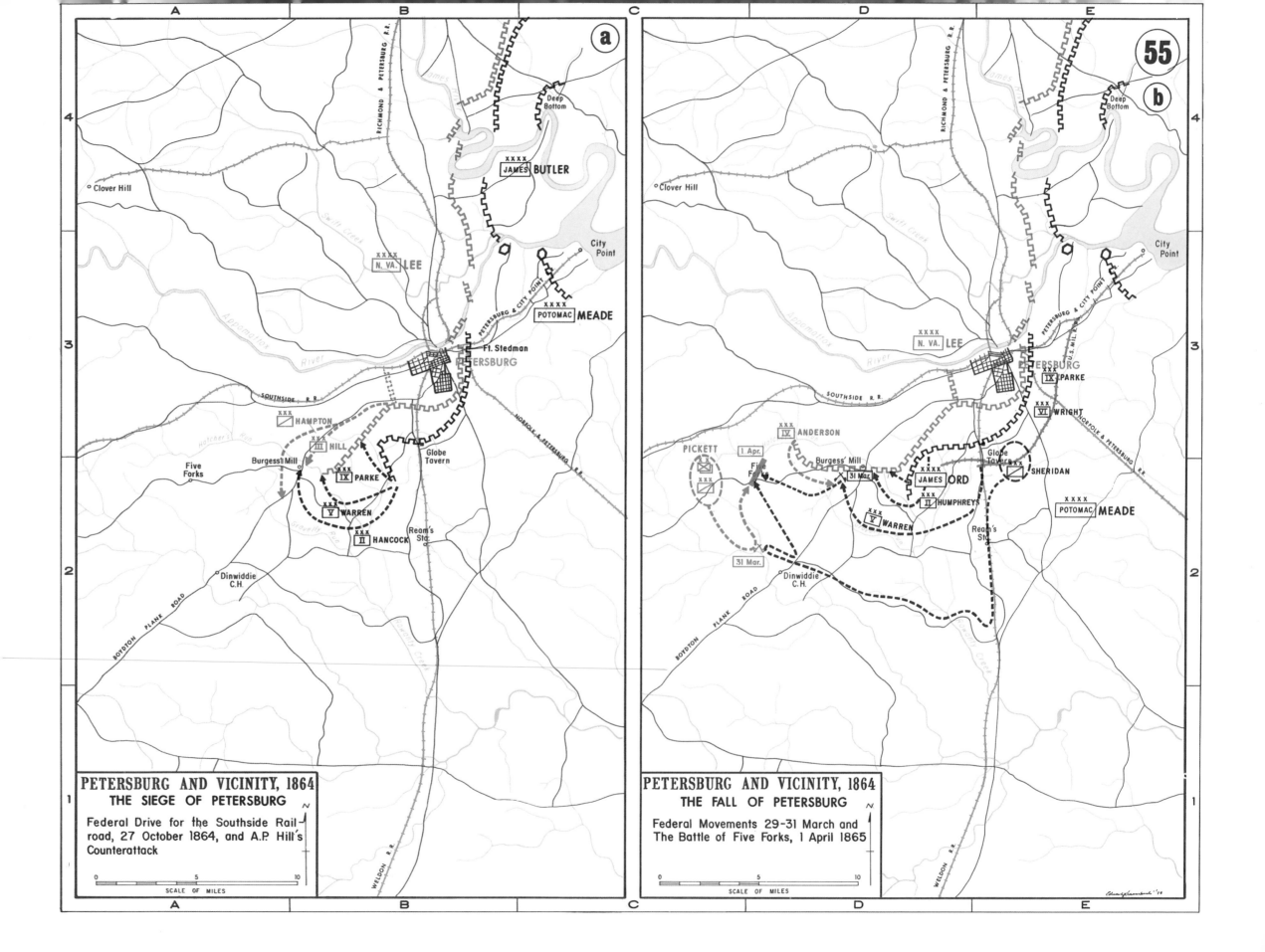

a

55

b

Deep Bottom

xxxx JAMES **BUTLER**

Clover Hill

City Point

xxxx N. VA. **LEE**

xxxx POTOMAC **MEADE**

Ft. Stedman

PETERSBURG

RICHMOND & PETERSBURG R.R.

PETERSBURG & CITY POINT

SOUTHSIDE R.R.

xxx **HAMPTON**

xxx **HILL**

Burgess' Mill

Globe Tavern

xxx IX **PARKE**

Five Forks

xxx V **WARREN**

NORFOLK & PETERSBURG R.R.

xxx II **HANCOCK**

Ream's Sta.

Dinwiddie C.H.

BOYDTON PLANK ROAD

WELDON R.R.

SCALE OF MILES

PETERSBURG AND VICINITY, 1864
THE SIEGE OF PETERSBURG

Federal Drive for the Southside Railroad, 27 October 1864, and A.P. Hill's
Counterattack

0   5   10

Deep Bottom

Clover Hill

City Point

xxx N. VA. **LEE**

PETERSBURG

IX **PARKE**

xxx VI **WRIGHT**

xxx IV **ANDERSON**

PICKETT

1 Apr.

Five Forks

31 Mar.

Burgess' Mill

Globe Tavern

SHERIDAN

xxxx JAMES **ORD**

xxx II **HUMPHREYS**

xxx V **WARREN**

Ream's Sta.

31 Mar.

xxxx POTOMAC **MEADE**

Dinwiddie C.H.

SOUTHSIDE R.R.

RICHMOND & PETERSBURG R.R.

PETERSBURG & CITY POINT

U.S. MIL. R.R.

BOYDTON PLANK ROAD

WELDON R.R.

SCALE OF MILES

PETERSBURG AND VICINITY, 1864
THE FALL OF PETERSBURG

Federal Movements 29-31 March and
The Battle of Five Forks, 1 April 1865

0   5   10

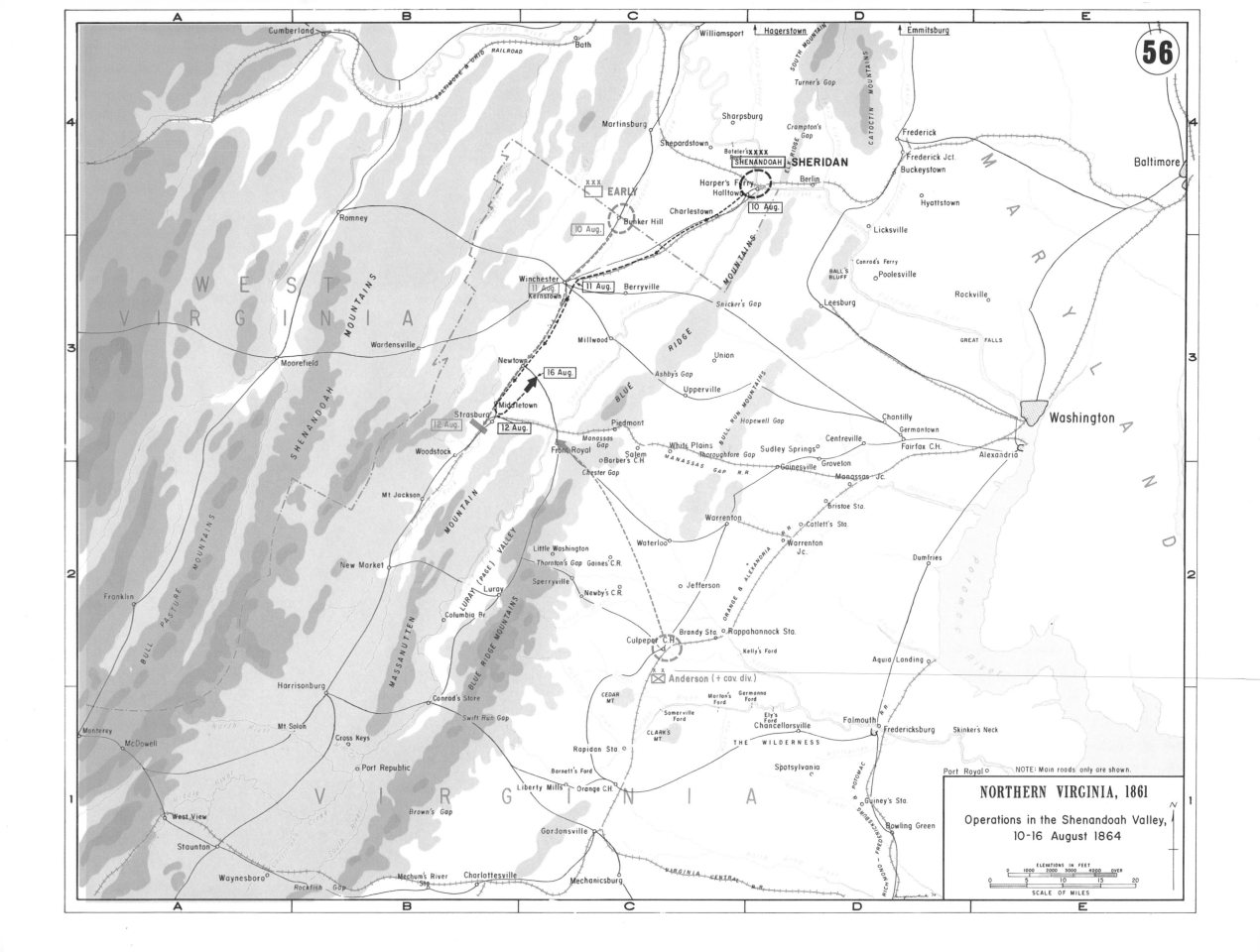

NORTHERN VIRGINIA, 1861

Operations in the Shenandoah Valley,
10-16 August 1864

NOTE: Main roads only are shown.

ELEVATIONS IN FEET
1000 2000 3000 4000 OVER

SCALE OF MILES

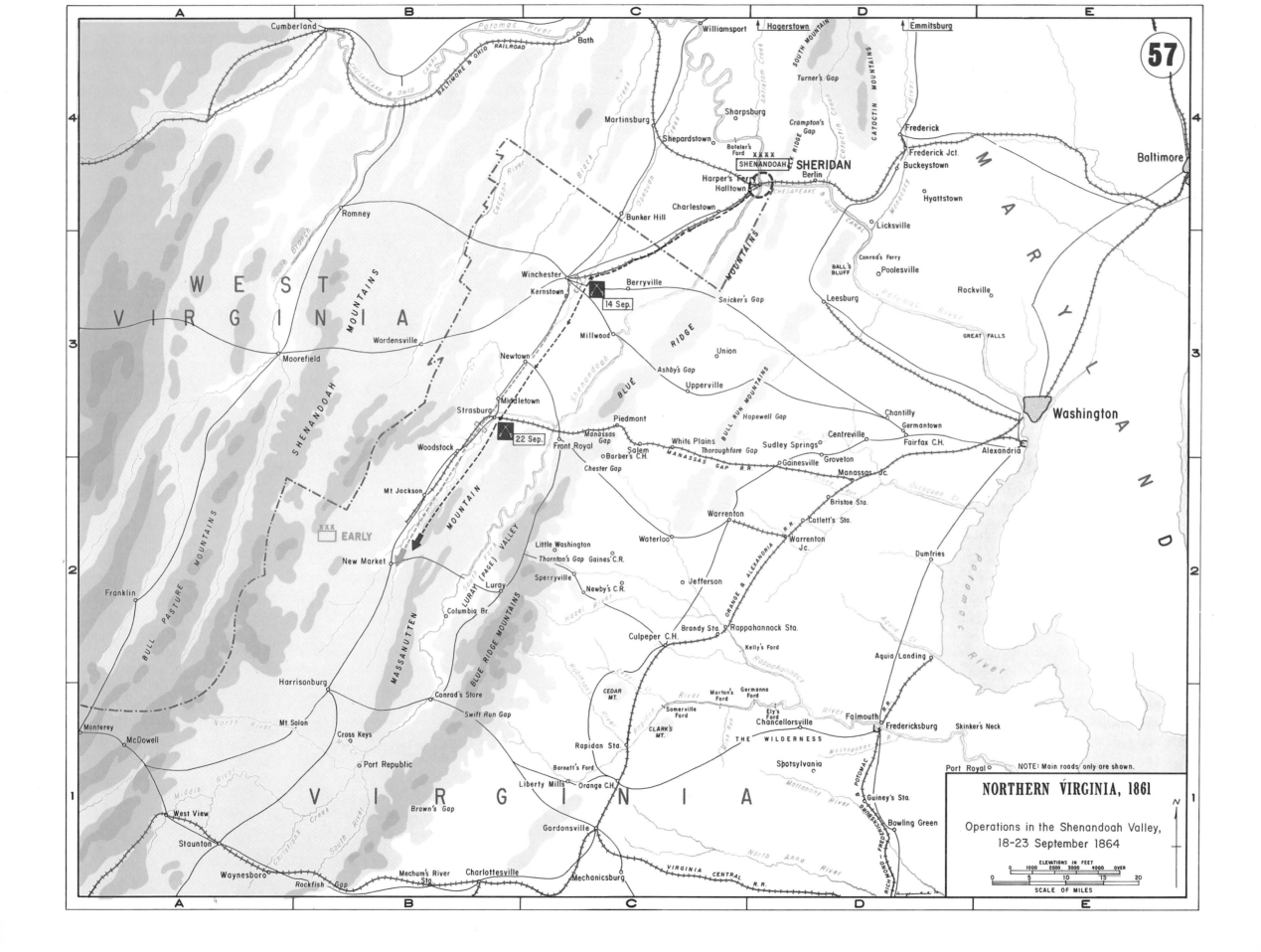

NORTHERN VIRGINIA, 1861

Operations in the Shenandoah Valley,
18-23 September 1864

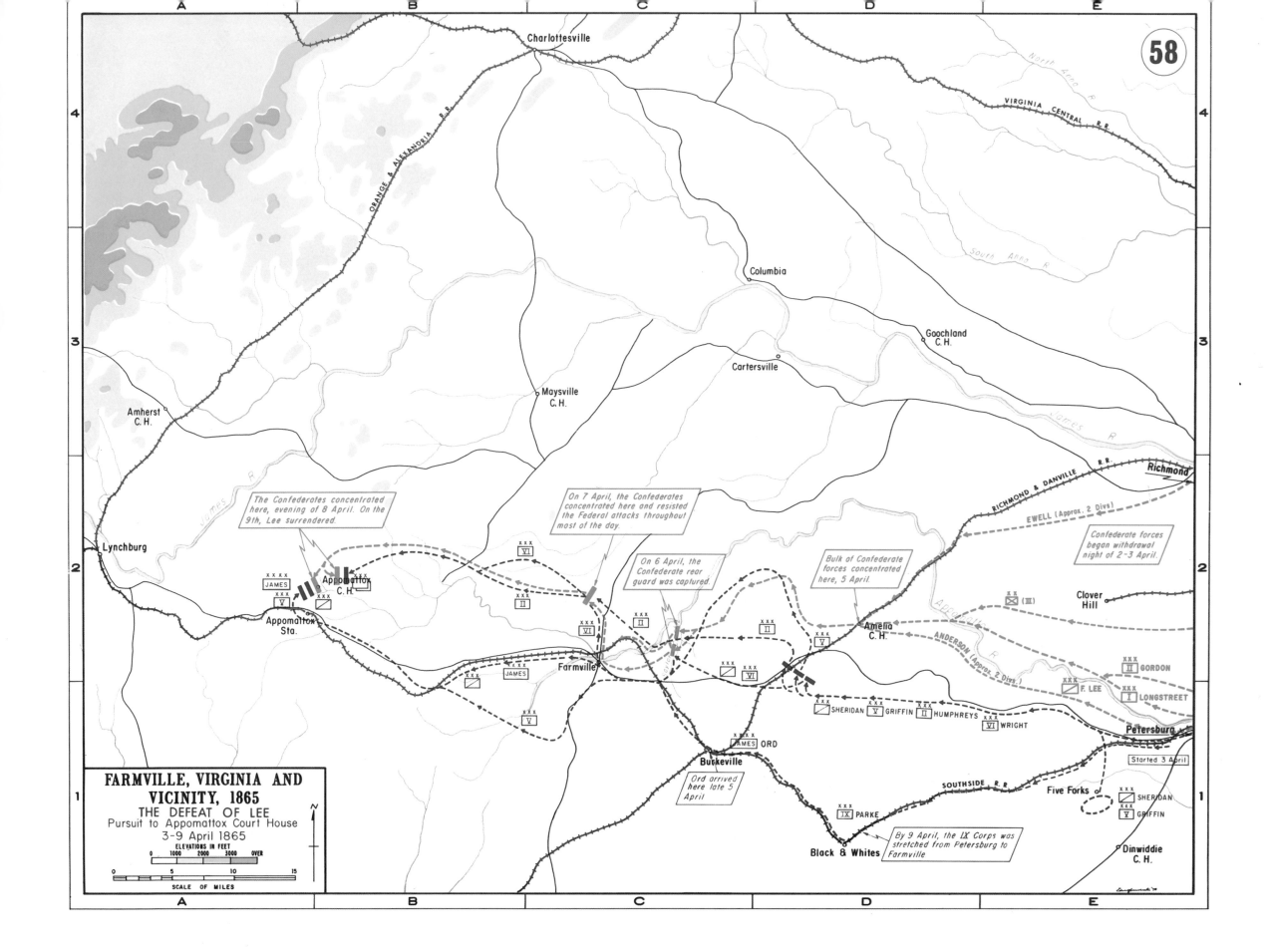

Charlottesville

VIRGINIA CENTRAL R.R.

North Anna R.

ORANGE & ALEXANDRIA R.R.

Columbia

South Anna R.

Goochland
C. H.

Cartersville

Maysville
C. H.

Amherst
C. H.

James R.

James R.

Richmond

RICHMOND & DANVILLE R.R.

The Confederates concentrated here, evening of 8 April. On the 9th, Lee surrendered.

On 7 April, the Confederates concentrated here and resisted the Federal attacks throughout most of the day.

EWELL (Approx. 2 Divs)

Confederate forces began withdrawal night of 2-3 April.

Lynchburg

On 6 April, the Confederate rear guard was captured.

Bulk of Confederate forces concentrated here, 5 April.

XXXX
JAMES

XXX
V

Appomattox
C. H.

XXX

Appomattox
Sta.

XXX
VI

XXX
II

XXX
VI

XXX
II

XXX
V

XXX
II

Amelia
C. H.

Appomattox R.

ANDERSON (Approx. 2 Divs)

Clover
Hill

(III)

XXX
II   GORDON

XXX
JAMES

XXX

XXX
VI

XXX
F. LEE

XXX
I   LONGSTREET

XXX   SHERIDAN

XXX
V   GRIFFIN

XXX
II   HUMPHREYS

XXX
VI   WRIGHT

Petersburg

XXX
V

JAMES   ORD

Started 3 April

SOUTHSIDE R.R.

Burkeville

Ord arrived here late 5 April

Five Forks

XXX
SHERIDAN

XXX
V   GRIFFIN

XXX
IX   PARKE

FARMVILLE, VIRGINIA AND VICINITY, 1865
THE DEFEAT OF LEE
Pursuit to Appomattox Court House
3-9 April 1865

ELEVATIONS IN FEET

0   1000   2000   3000   OVER

0   5   10   15

SCALE OF MILES

N

By 9 April, the IX Corps was stretched from Petersburg to Farmville

Black & Whites

Dinwiddie
C. H.